They had to deal with the situation as it was now. They had little food, a young Red was being held against his will *and* against the ancient Kernel Lore, the land was being overrun by Greys of the Second Wave, all seemingly under the influence of the Temple Master, and on top of this, Tansy was constantly pressing her to go to the aid of the squirrels on Ourland. So many things to be considered and no clear line of action to be seen.

They had reached the edge of the hollow in which the Blue Pool lay. The surface was calm in the late-winter sunshine and the upside-down reflections of the Beachend trees were green against the blue of the mirrored sky. Even in her agitated state Marguerite felt the surge of joy that always came when she looked at the loveliness of the pool and its setting. The Sun forbid that she would ever have to leave it again. Yet somehow she knew it would come to that.

Michael Tod was born in 1937 in Dorset, where this story is set. He lived near Weymouth until his family moved to a hill farm in Wales when he was eleven. His childhood experiences on the Dorset coast and in the Welsh mountains have given him a deep love and knowledge of wild creatures and the countryside, which is reflected in his poetry and fiction and inspired *The Woodstock Saga*. Married, with three children and three grandchildren, he still lives, works and walks in his beloved Welsh hills, but visits his old haunts in Dorset whenever he can.

BY THE SAME AUTHOR

The Silver Tide
The Golden Flight

THE SECOND WAVE

MICHAEL TOD

An Orion paperback
First published in Great Britain in 1994 by Orion
This paperback edition published in 1995 by Orion Books Ltd,
Orion House, 5 Upper St Martin's Lane, London WC2H 9EA

A CIP catalogue record for this book is available from the British Library.

ISBN: 1 85797 740 8

Printed in England by Clays Ltd, St Ives plc

To the Misled

This is a work of fiction. Names, characters and incidents are either the product of the author's imagination or used fictitiously (such as the rededication of the church on Brownsea Island). Any resemblance to actual events, people or squirrels is entirely coincidental.

Maps

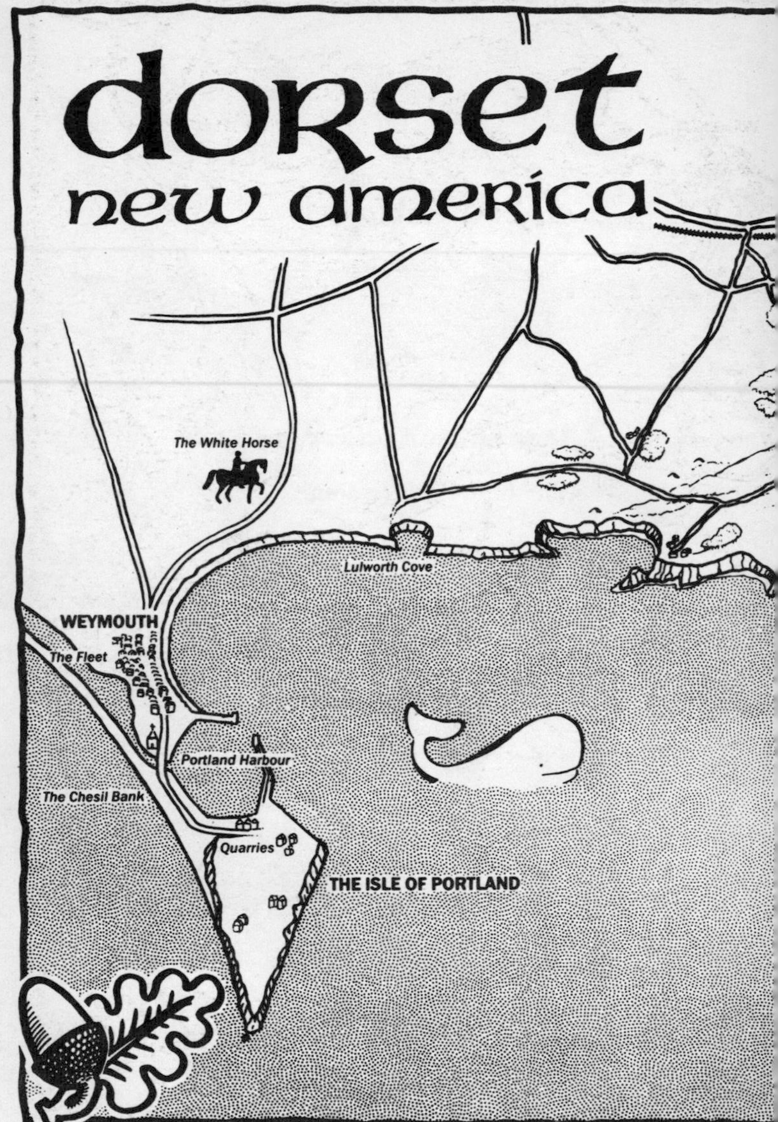
dorset
new america
The White Horse
Lulworth Cove
WEYMOUTH
The Fleet
Portland Harbour
The Chesil Bank
Quarries
THE ISLE OF PORTLAND

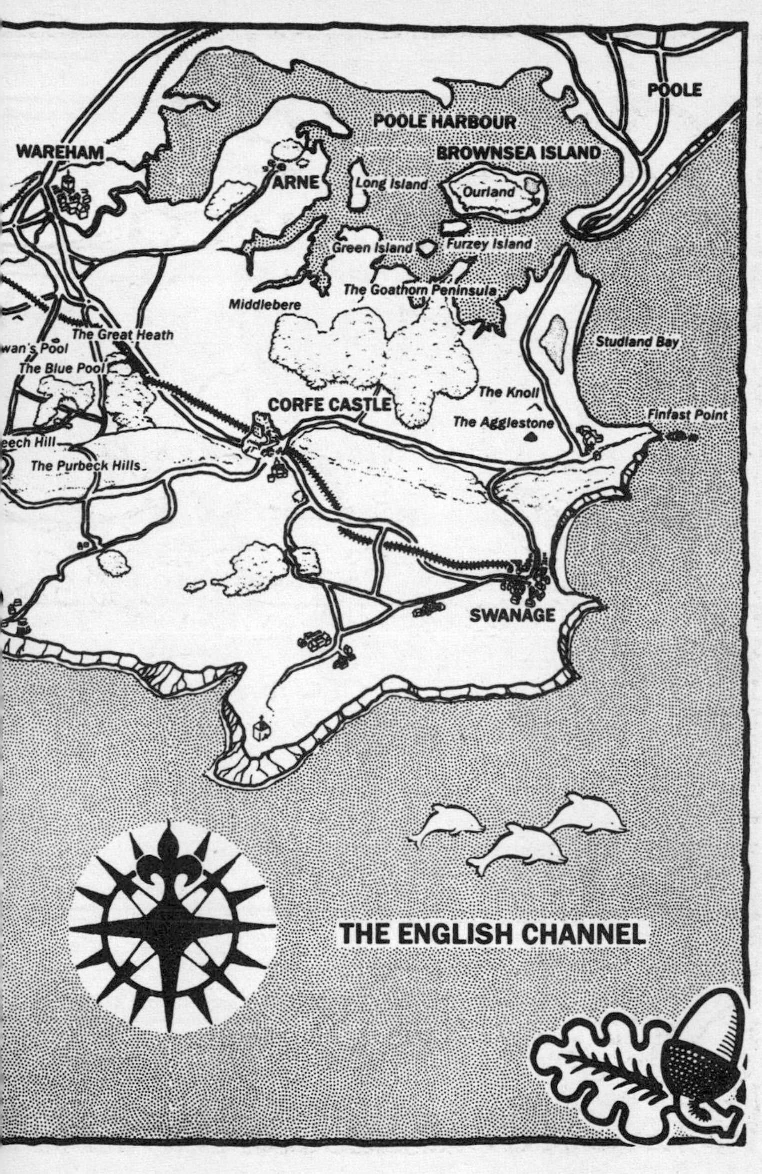
POOLE
POOLE HARBOUR
WAREHAM
BROWNSEA ISLAND
ARNE
Long Island
Ourland
Green Island
Furzey Island
The Goathorn Peninsula
Middlebere
The Great Heath
wan's Pool
The Blue Pool
Studland Bay
The Knoll
CORFE CASTLE
The Agglestone
Finfast Point
eech Hill
The Purbeck Hills
SWANAGE
THE ENGLISH CHANNEL

Characters

RED SQUIRRELS OF PORTLAND

Crag the Temple Master; his mate *Rusty*; their son *Chip*

RED SQUIRRELS OF THE BLUE POOL DEMESNE

Alder the Leader; his life-mate *Dandelion* the Storyteller
Juniper the Steadfast; his life-mate *Marguerite* the Tagger
Rowan the Bold; his life-mate *Meadowsweet* Rowan's Love
Spindle the Helpful; his life-mate *Wood Anemone* the Able
Dreylings and youngsters of the above
Tamarisk the Forthright

RED SQUIRRELS OF OURLAND

EX-ROYALS

Ex-King *Willow*; his mate Ex-Kingz-Mate *Thizle*; their son *Just Poplar*; their daughter *Teazle*; their nephew *Fir*; their nieces *Voxglove* and *Cowzlip*

EX-ZERVANTZ

Bug
Beetle
Caterpiller
Maple (was *Maggot*)

INCOMERS

Oak the Cautious; his life-mate *Fern* the Fussy
Larch the Curious; his life-mate *Clover* the Tagger and Carer; their daughter *Tansy* the Wistful
Chestnut the Doubter; his life-mate *Heather* Treetops

GREY SQUIRRELS OF THE SECOND WAVE

Ivy, or *Poison Ivy* (was *Slate*)
Redwood (was *Basalt*)
Hickory (was *Chalk*)
Sitka (was *Shale*)
Bluegrass (was *Tufa*)
Yucca
Prairie Rose
Other unnamed survivors of the Grey Death

OTHERS

Blood the pine marten
Mogul the peacock; his harem of peahens
Malin the dolphin; his mate *Lundy*; their son *Finisterre*
Acorn and *Primrose,* the mythical first squirrels in the world

Chapter 1

1962

Chip sat on top of the world. At least, that was what it seemed like to him as he looked down from the edge of the cliff. The wind was chill and he wriggled back into the shelter of a rock.

"Squimp!" called Crag, his father, in a voice as cold as the wind which tore at his fur. "Out from behind that rock. Now!"

Chip, a thin, first-year red squirrel, came out reluctantly and crouched beside his mother, Rusty, keeping as far away as he could from Crag, the Temple Master. He could never be sure of when he would get a cuff across the back of his head and it was as well to stay out of his father's reach.

He stood up and followed the gaze of his parents as they studied the panorama below, a gust buffeting him and tugging at his pointed ears where the first tufts were just beginning to show. The squirrels were on the very edge of the north-western cliff-top of Portland. Below him the white stone cliff-face fell away to terraces of tumbled rocks, against which the dark green, gale-driven sea fretted and gnawed. As he watched, a great wave crashed and tore itself to pieces in a weltering mass of foam and spray.

Looking further northwards, his eyes followed the golden sweep of the Chesil Beach curving away into the far distance, the September sun glowing on the myriad high-banked pebbles protecting the Fleet Lagoon which lay between the pebble bank and the land. Beyond his father, on his right-paw side, over the jostle of Man-dens on the lower ground, he could see the blue sheltered waters of Portland Harbour where battleships lay at anchor, but Young Chip had no idea what these were. A squirrel youngster has much to learn about the world, especially if he is the only one of his year on the great stone mass which is the Isle of Portland, so windswept that trees are rare, surviving only in hollows and a few other sheltered places.

He watched the blue of the harbour turn to grey as gusts of wind rippled the surface, then as the gold of the Chesil Beach darkened, he looked to his left. A bank of clouds had covered the sun and was racing towards the land trailing a grey veil below it. He knew that in a few minutes a rain squall would reach them, and again turned instinctively for cover. Crag glowered at him, so he turned back, to stare miserably out to sea, shivering. Even the comfortless stone of their den in the cave at the back of the quarry had been preferable to this!

Chip's world had suddenly changed with the death of his grandfather, Old Sarsen, five days before.

Chip had been with his parents in the Temple Cave, crouched near a mass of rusting scrap iron where the old squirrel lay, wheezing and coughing out his last instructions to Crag and Rusty.

"Remember your vows," the old squirrel had said. "*You* are nothing. The Sun is everything. Worship and serve it, or it'll be the Sunless Pit for both of you. For ever!"

Chip could still hear the intensity of expression in his grandfather's voice. "You there, you, young one, remember this – serve the Sun. The Sun is everything. Fear the Sun and *dread* the Sunless Pit."

Chip could recall the shudders of terror which had engulfed him. The thought of never seeing the sun again had terrified him, and even now his stomach churned with the thought.

"You will all have to leave Portland," his grandfather had told them. "The Sun punished all unworthy squirrels by denying them dreylings. They were too idle to collect the sacred metal as we all do, so the Sun in its wisdom denied them issue. There are only four of us left here now and the youngster will need to mate next year. Go to the Mainland. Carry the True Word. Serve the Sun."

"What about the Temple?" Crag had asked.

"You will have to leave it. It will still be here if you can ever return."

The old squirrel had scrabbled at the stone floor, his blunt claws slipping on the rock, worn smooth by the feet of generations of his ancestors, until with one last effort he had hauled himself to the top of the pile of metal, the rattle of empty tins echoing around the hollow of the cave. Then, in the silence that followed, he called,

"Sun, I've served you well.
Take me to you. Save me from –
That dread Sunless Pit!"

An agonised look had crossed his face and his lifeless body had tumbled down the pile to sprawl at Chip's feet.

Showing no trace of emotion, Crag had ordered Rusty and Chip to help him drag the scraggy body up the rock face, to one of the drill holes left when the quarry was abandoned, where they had slid it, head first, down the hole, to join the bones of Old Sarsen's father and those of his father before him.

Death must be as uncomfortable as life if a squirrel was to avoid the Sunless Pit, the youngster had thought.

A seagull whirled past Chip's head, squawking as it was tossed on the updraught of the wind striking the cliff-face, and a kestrel that had been hovering turned away inland and dropped between the mass of rocks behind them. Out over the sea, the rain clouds were much nearer.

"We go down," Crag ordered.

Chip gave a last look at the wrinkled sea below and at where the waves twisted over themselves as they ran along the curve of the Chesil Beach, then followed his parents on to the vertical face of the rock.

The wind buffeted him, but he climbed down head-first, confidently finding claw-holds in the tiniest of cracks and crevices. As Mainland squirrels were totally at home in trees, so was he on rock; neither he nor any of his family had ever climbed a tree.

He had once seen a tattered sycamore in a sheltered hollow whilst searching for metal with his grandfather and had moved towards it, drawn by this exciting living thing which created such a strange craving within him, but Old Sarsen had ordered him to leave it alone. "Shut your eyes to the temptation," he had been told. "We will search this way", and the old squirrel had led the youngster off between the rocks away from the sin-provoking tree.

These long-abandoned quarries, though eerie places to humans, were quite familiar to Chip and his family. Huge blocks of substandard rock had been stacked in heaps, or scattered about as though by the paws of some giant squirrel, and over and around these wild cotoneaster bushes trailed, their green foliage now covered by blood-red berries. Large snails, their grey shells banded with a darker whirl, grazed on the leaves, and grasshoppers, safe here from lowland farmers' pesticides, chirred and chirruped amongst the yellow-flowered ragwort and the purple valerian. Above the squirrels the spiky dry seed-heads of teazles had patterned the skyline.

In the quarry-waste they had found an old pick head, flaking into layers of rust, but, despite the combined efforts of the old squirrel and the youngster, they had been unable to do more than drag it to the bottom of the cliff below the Temple Cave. There they had had to leave it, lying amongst the hart's tongue ferns, a constant reminder of how feeble they were, compared with the might of the Sun above.

A moon or so ago Chip had asked his mother about the metal collecting. At first she had seemed reluctant to speak of it. Then, when just the two of them were out searching and had found nothing, she had spoken unguardedly in frustration.

"I'm sure the Sun doesn't want all this stuff," she had said. "It was your great-grandfather, Monolith, who started it all. He was the chief of all the Portland squirrels then, and a miserable old creature by all accounts. I never found out what sin he did that was so awful that he thought he had to punish himself this way. Metal collecting is a bore and it hurts our teeth and I hate the whole stupid business.

"Even worse, he taught your grandfather to do it and he taught your father. Now *he's* teaching you. When will it ever stop? Why in the name of the Sun do *we* have to suffer for something Old Monolith did that everyone has forgotten long ago?"

Chip had stared at his mother. She had never spoken like this before; he did not know what to say.

Rusty continued, the words tumbling out. "My brother, your uncle, said that the problem with living isolated on islands is that extreme ideas get more and more exaggerated."

Chip had wondered what "exaggerated" meant. He raised his tail into the query position and was about to ask, when his mother said, "He died last year with no dreylings to follow him. I do miss him."

Rusty had looked tired and worn, and Chip had moved across to comfort her, but she had waved him away.

"I shouldn't have said that," she had told him. "For the Sun's sake, and mine, don't repeat it. Come on, we must find *something*."

They had searched all day, quartering the stone slabs of the quarry floor, raking with their claws through every tuft of grass and peering into each crack and hole between the stones, but had returned to the cave with only a crown cap from a discarded bottle between them, to the disgust of Old Sarsen, the Temple Master.

Once Chip had complained that it hurt his teeth to drag

rusty tins along the stony paths of the old quarries, and the stern old squirrel had said, "That's one of the reasons why we do it. The discomfort is good for you."

Everything that felt uncomfortable, it seemed, was "good for you". The bundle of dried grass that he had once brought into the cave to make the ground less hard to sleep on had been thrown out, and he had been called "a self-indulgent squimp". He was *glad* the old squirrel was gone, but now his father seemed to be just as awful!

Crag, Rusty and Chip doggedly worked their way down the cliff-face, one paw searching for a new hold whilst the other three held on to whatever projection or crack their sharp claws could cling to. Crag and Chip moved confidently, heads down, but Rusty, never happy on high faces, descended slowly, tail first, feeling for holds and keeping her teeth clamped tightly together. It would not do to show fear.

Chip called out to her, "There's a good hold just below your left paw", but his words were lost in the splash and roar as the rain squall reached the land, drenching the squirrels on the rock face. In a moment their wet fur flattened to their skins and their tails became as thin as those of rats.

"Hold on," shouted Crag. "It'll pass in a moment."

They clung to the rock face chilled and uncomfortable, Rusty's teeth chattering audibly. Then, as suddenly as it had arrived, the squall passed on and the sun was visible again, though now so low that little warmth reached the cliff-bound animals. Crag signalled them to start down again.

*

The light was fading from the western sky as the three reached the tumbled rocks piled along the cliff-base. Here there was some protection from the wind, and the bedraggled animals hopped down from rock to rock, making their way towards the shore.

Chip could hear the crashing of the waves above the roar of the wind and a melancholy whistling as the gusts tore through the brambles and the shrubby bushes which grew between the fallen rocks. He shivered and kept close behind his mother, hoping his father would stop soon. He was cold and hungry, and this unfamiliar place frightened him.

As the last of the daylight died they came to a Man-den, a wooden hut built between two great rocks, where his father and mother sniffed the air for recent scents. Then, apparently satisfied, Chip's father wriggled into the darkness underneath the hut's wooden floor.

"This'll do for us," he called back, and Rusty and Chip crawled in after him.

Compared with the outside world, it was warm under the hut floor and the youngster licked himself dry; he could hear his parents doing the same. He was very hungry, but knew better than to ask for food, which plainly wasn't to be had that night. He would have to wait until morning, so he fumbled about in the darkness for a sleeping place. In a corner he found a pile of dry grass brought in by some other animal, and quietly and guiltily burrowed into it. He knew this was a sinful act, but he was *so* cold. No squirrel would know, but he must remember to be lying on the bare ground before it got light.

He heard his father start the Evening Prayer.

Invincible Sun,
Forgive us, your poor squirrels,
For always failing.

Tomorrow, we will,
If you will give us the strength,
Try to do better.

Try to do better at what? Chip wondered. What would the Mainland be like? Would they find other squirrels? Would they be like he was? There were so many questions that he dared not ask. He wriggled round in the grass and slept restlessly.

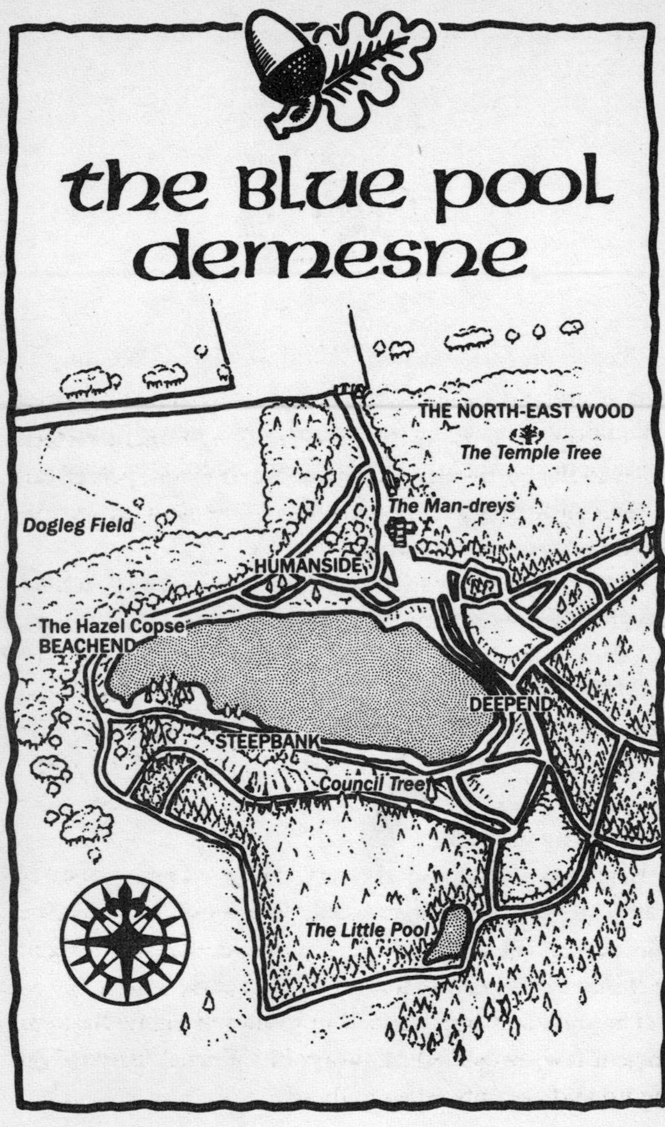
the Blue pool demesne
THE NORTH-EAST WOOD
The Temple Tree
The Man-dreys
Dogleg Field
HUMANSIDE
The Hazel Copse
BEACHEND
DEEPEND
STEEPBANK
Council Tree
The Little Pool

Chapter 2

The rain and the wind had died away during the night and the red squirrels at the Blue Pool, on the Mainland fifteen miles to the north-east of Portland's great rock, peered out of their snug dreys at the pink glow in the sky that was the herald of a warm autumn day.

Alder the Leader had declared this day was to be a Sunday, devoted to fun and recreation.

Even as early as this the squirrels could sense the squirrelation that would spread from drey to drey and bring them all together to enjoy each other's company, with feasting, chases through the branches and, in the dusk, story-telling in the Council Tree on the steep bank overlooking the pool.

Each knew that the Harvest was in. Their weeks of frantic activity were over, and sufficient nuts were hidden and buried to see them through the hardest of winters and well into the otherwise hungry days of early spring.

The nuts had been hidden in groups of eight. By their ancient law, embodied as always in a Kernel, they would dig up and eat only seven of these.

One out of eight nuts
Must be left to germinate.
Here grows our future.

Marguerite the Tagger paused with her head outside and her body still in the warmth of the drey high in the Deepend tree. She sniffed the air and pulled her head inside. There was time for another little doze. Her two youngsters, Burdock and Oak, were big enough to fend for themselves. Together with the other squirrels born that year, they had been Tagged at her recommendation with an appropriate Tag to indicate their character, or to commemorate some worthy, or unworthy, achievement.

To be a True Tagger demanded a great deal of observation and concentration. An unfair denigratory tag could ruin a squirrel's life, though there would always be a chance to earn a better one. This year had produced a good-quality harvest of dreylings. One was her own son, Young Oak, who had earned his tag, the Wary, because he was always suspiciously alert for any sense of danger. Marguerite's father, Oak, Young Oak's grandfather, was tagged the Cautious, and some squirrels thought that the two tags meant the same thing, but, to a True Tagger, there was a world of difference. It was a good thing to have a "wary" son; it meant that there was a better chance of grandchildren. Being Wary was a good trait.

Her brother, Rowan the Bold, lived at the humans' side of the pool. His tag had been with him since he was a dreyling and suited him well, though now as a father of two he could not indulge in exciting climbabout journeys away from the Blue Pool any more. Marguerite was sure that he missed these and that he sometimes fretted at the lack of opportunity to be bold and adventurous.

One of her short-lived uncles, Beech, had earned the tag the Ant Watcher from his obsessive fascination with the way wood-ants carried food to their nests under huge mounds of pine needles. Beech had been watching a little group of seven ants cooperating to move a dead caterpillar when the fox had seen him. The Ant Watcher had not even felt the snap of its jaws.

Marguerite's daughter, Young Burdock, had been tagged the Thoughtful. Like Marguerite herself, she was always trying to puzzle out complex things. Marguerite recalled her own early tag, the Bright One, and wanting to know exactly to what it referred; but even then she had known that it was bad form to question your tag.

Now, with the two youngsters chattering excitedly on the branch outside, she gave up any hope of a doze and nudged her life-mate, Juniper the Steadfast, to wake him.

It had taken him a long time to earn *that* tag. He was two years her senior, and she had never even known his first tag. It had been the Scavenger when she was a dreyling, then the Swimmer after an incident with the invading grey squirrels the year before. Finally, he had earned his present tag by always being reliably at her side through all the dangers and hazards they had experienced together since his first life-mate, Bluebell, had given her life to save others. Bluebell was the only squirrel to have had a tag-change after death; she was awarded the tag Who Gave All to Save Us in place of Who Sold Herself for Peanuts, which had been earned by behaviour they all wanted to forget.

Marguerite wriggled out of the drey, sat on a branch and

groomed herself in the sunshine, licking her fur and combing her tail hairs with her claws. Soon Juniper followed her.

"Perfect day for a Sun-day," he said, looking round at the tops of the pine trees where the rain-soaked needles were steaming away the night's moisture, then down to the pool, which he could glimpse through the tree-trunks below. He sat there, as he did on most fine mornings, combing his whiskers and enjoying the colour of the pool. It was a different colour every day. Sometimes, as now, it would be blue. On other mornings it would start green and change through several shades of turquoise and eau-de-Nil. Even on overcast days it usually ended up that intense sapphire colour that had earned it the Blue tag and which attracted humans to come and see it summer after summer.

Marguerite and her family climbed head first down the trunk of their tree to forage, pausing below branch level to look about and scent for possible danger. Juniper spoke the Kernel:

A watchful squirrel
Survives to breed and father –
More watchful squirrels.

Kernels as important as this one could not be repeated too often. Knowing these gave the youngsters the greatest chance of survival in a world in which a squirrel would be regarded by many animals as nothing more than a welcome meal.

It is so peaceful here, now that the Greys have gone, Marguerite was thinking. So pleasant to live quietly in this beautiful place with her life-mate and their youngsters after the frenetic action of the previous two years. And yet . . . No, she didn't really enjoy all that activity, and yet . . . She had to admit to herself that it was exciting having to plan for your very survival, using your wits, and your energy and skills, to keep one leap ahead of your enemies . . .

Chapter 3

Chip woke with a start. It was still dark, but he knew he must be out of the warmth of the dried grass before his parents discovered that he had sinned by indulging himself with comfort. He thought there was a little time yet before his parents would wake, so he wriggled down again into the warm nest. The storm must have blown itself out. There was no wind-sound, though he could feel vibrations through the ground from the sea-swell pounding the rocky shoreline.

He lay there, listening to the breathing of his sleeping parents, trying to identify an unfamiliar feeling that surrounded him. He tried to focus on it, straining his mind and his whiskers to pick up whatever it was. In a way it resembled the warmth of the grass around his body, but it was more subtle than that. It came from the wood above him, from the Man-den, the hut on its little plateau amongst the huge boulders.

There were no men there – he would have scented and heard them moving long before this – but it *was* Man-associated. It was something like the "cared for" feeling he remembered from his mother when she had suckled him back in the spring. Then, in a distant, painful memory, he recalled his grandfather, Old Sarsen, saying, "Don't get squimpish about that youngster. He's not yours. You have only borne him to serve the Sun." And over the next few days that warm, cared-for feeling had been withdrawn.

Now he sensed that the hut was cared for, by humans. Could *things* be cared for? Could squirrels themselves ever be cared for except when they were dreylings? He hugged himself with the excitement of the thought.

A finger of grey light probed under the hut. Chip quietly destroyed his nest in the corner and moved away from the scattered grass to lie down on the cold soil until his parents woke. They lay as they taught him to, with their tails away from their bodies so as not to indulge in the warmth these might unworthily give them. He copied them and shivered.

A herring-gull, perched on the ridge of the hut above, called raucously. Crag and Rusty sat up at the same time and Rusty reached out and shook her son's shoulder where he lay, pretending to be asleep. "Time for prayers, Chip-Son," she told him.

Crag glowered at her.

"Chip, you must wake now," she said, forcing herself to sound hard and uncaring.

The three went out into the chill of the dawn air. If the sun *was* up over the eastern sea, it was hidden by the vast stone bulk of Portland behind them. Crag climbed on to a small rock, gave a quick look round for danger and, seeing none, said the Morning Prayer:

Be not too wrathful,
Oh Great Sun, on those squirrels –
Who sinned in the night.

Chip shifted uncomfortably as Crag went on.

Let us serve your needs
For the whole of this your day
Weak though we may be.

"Let us find sustenance," Crag said, after the long silence that followed, and only then could they start to forage amongst the rocks for food.

On the seaward side of the hut a spring of clear water trickled down through small pools overhung with brambles. Each drank from the stream in turn; first Crag, then Rusty, then Chip.

They found a few roots and a puffball which, though beginning to set spores, was just edible. These, with a few hard-pipped blackberries and some crimson hips, made up their meagre breakfast. Then Crag saw some sloes on a stunted blackthorn bush between two rocks and allowed each of them one of the mouth-drying fruit, before ordering Rusty and Chip to follow him along a Man-track that wound between the boulders.

The light was stronger now and Chip could see many more of the wooden Man-dens between the rocks. Most were brightly coloured and radiated that odd cared-for feeling he had sensed during the night, but a few were dilapidated and forlorn, the wood unpainted and weathered grey, their doors and windows hanging open or broken.

None of the huts appeared to be occupied. Maybe the humans used them only in the summer, Chip thought, as Crag hurried them on. His shoulder brushed against a plant with brown-edged leaves that leaned over the path, and little hooked seeds clung to his fur. He stopped to try to comb them out, but burdocks had evolved the tiny hooks to take their seeds well away from the parent plants, and they were not easy to remove.

Seeing that Chip had stopped, Crag called back over his shoulder, "Keep going. We must avoid meeting humans. They are trouble, and their dogs will chase us."

The sun cleared the top of the cliffs as they hopped along the path which wound in and out, up and down, through the tumbled boulders, and more and more Man-signs were to be seen. Wet paper bags and stinking cigarette-ends littered the sides of the Man-track. Chip found a rusty nail and showed it to Crag, expecting him to collect it as they usually did for the Temple, but was brusquely told, "We'll have to leave it."

His father did, however, pick it up and hide it out of human sight.

Rounding the last of the rocks at the end of the path, they could see ahead of them rows of stone Man-dens ranged behind the great bank of pebbles that curved away into the distance. Crag signalled to them to lie low whilst he climbed up on to a large boulder to plan a route. When he re-joined them, he led them away from the track and down on to the beach.

The smooth round stones here were bigger than the squirrels themselves, and they hopped from one stone to another, keeping on the seaward side of the debris forming the high-tide line.

Chip wanted to stop and look. Huge rollers, a legacy of the previous day's storm, towered in the air before crashing down in a mass of foam and rushing up the beach as though intent on snatching the animals and dragging them down into the depths. Then the waves, losing their momentum, drew back over the stones, which rubbed and tumbled against each other, groaning like a great beast in its death throes, only to be tossed forward yet again. But Crag, with that familiar "nothing will stop me now" look in his eye, urged them on.

After they passed the Man-dens and some brightly painted boats drawn up on the beach, there was nothing on their right-paw side between them and the sky but the top of the pebble bank, whilst to their left the empty sea stretched away to a far horizon. They hurried on, and Portland, well behind them now, appeared smaller each time they glanced back.

Chip was hungry again.

It got harder and harder to make progress along the beach. The pebbles were smaller now, about the size of a squirrel's head, and each rolled underfoot in a way that quickly tired their legs. Rusty called to Crag, "It might be easier if we followed that line of seaweed." She indicated the high-tide mark.

"Things are not meant to be easy," Crag told her.

"If we were not slipping about so, I think we could make better time. Old Sarsen said we were to leave Portland and it is our *duty* to go as quickly as we can. That's all I meant," she added lamely, as Crag glowered at her.

"Very well," he conceded. "But try to keep up with me. Both of you!"

They hopped up the beach and then from one clump of seaweed to the next, clambering over twisted pieces of smooth grey driftwood and splintered spars and old planks tossed up by the sea. Chip wanted to sense and examine all of them, but Crag kept urging them on. The waves to their left continually rushed up the beach, churning the pebbles, grinding them ever smaller.

"Don't hang back," Crag growled over his shoulder when Chip stopped and sniffed at the oil-soaked feathers of a dead guillemot. Chip reached out, however, and touched the sticky black stuff covering the bird before scrambling on after his parents.

Some of the black stuff had stuck to his paw, so he rubbed it on his belly-fur to try to clean it. Looking down, he could see that the stuff was now there as well. He tried to lick it off, but the taste was foul on his tongue.

"Don't lag behind," Crag shouted back to him, and Chip hurried to catch up, leaving a grey mark on every pebble that his paw touched. The smell of the oil was now making him feel ill.

At High Sun Crag called a halt when he found the dried-up body of a dogfish. He thanked the Sun for providing them with unsought sustenance and the three of them gnawed through the rough skin to the stinking, crisp meat within. Chip ate only a little, still feeling queasy, then wandered away from his parents to poke about amongst the strange and fascinating stones and wood.

He was holding up a pebble with a hole right through it when his eye was caught by a glint from a disc of bright metal near his feet. He picked it up. It was as golden as the sun and as round as a pebble one way, but thin and flat the other. He turned it over in his paws. It had been smoothed by rubbing against the pebbles, but he could see that there was a human's head on one side and strange squiggles and shapes on the other. He showed it first to his mother, Rusty, then to Crag, who bit it with his sharp teeth. "Soft and useless metal," he pronounced. "No gift for the Sun!" Throwing the golden coin down the beach, he told them to follow him again.

After another mile of tiring progress Crag led the weary squirrels to the top of the ridge. Beyond them was the lagoon that they had first seen from the cliff-top. It separated the pebble bank from the green fields of the Mainland, though at one place they could see that the lagoon narrowed near a stone Man-den, and the box-things that humans travelled in were passing over the water at that point.

Crag decided that they would go that way and led them down from the ridge. Chip was pleased when they reached an area where the ground was flatter, and the pebbles, bound together with clay, no longer rolled underfoot. Tufty sea-pink, sea campion and other shoreline vegetation was growing between the stones in the hard ground and a huge hare, disturbed by the squirrels, rushed out of its form and lolloped up the beach and on to the loose pebbles, which rattled and clattered behind its enormous back feet.

The air chilled as the sun dropped behind the pebble bank. Chip hoped that they would soon stop so that he could rest at last, with a warm place to sleep, but Crag had other ideas. He kept urging his tired family on until they came to the wide, smooth Man-track which smelt like the stuff on the guillemot's feathers, and where the humans' box-things rushed along. The squirrels crouched, waiting in the dusk, until the roadway was clear, then scurried across it and down through the wiry grass of the bank on the far side. They found themselves in a large hollow amongst the hulking shapes of boats and many new and interesting smells.

Some of the boats were on the ground, others up on trailers ready to be towed away for winter storage. The squirrels prowled round the unfamiliar objects, vainly trying to work out what they were. The scent of dogs was faint on the grass but nauseatingly strong on the wheels of the boat trailers, even though some hours old. Crag set out to find a safe sleeping place as high above the ground as he could.

A rope hung from the bow of a sailing cruiser cradled in its trailer near the road. Crag caught at this as it swung in the wind and climbed up it to the deck. A mast was lashed horizontally on top of the cabin, and from this he called down to Rusty and Chip to follow him. They chased the evasive rope-end and clambered up to join him, whilst he nosed about until he found a gap under the cabin door large enough for them to squeeze through. It was warm inside the cabin and Chip hopped up on to a soft seat, only to be ordered down to the wooden floor.

"Don't indulge yourself, young one," Crag growled.

As darkness fell, the pungent smell of the oil on Chip's fur filled the airless confines of the cabin and they were all bothered by the swish, swish, swish of the cars passing on the road alongside them. In the early hours of the morning these sounds died away, but were soon replaced by the slap,

slap, slap of ropes against the masts of other craft nearby when a night wind rose and eddied about in the hollow where the boats were resting.

Chapter 4

The first glow of dawn was showing in the eastern sky beyond Portland Harbour when the squirrels in the boat were wakened by the sound of human voices outside. Crag hopped up on to one of the cabin seats and peered out through the round glass into the grey light. The largest travelling-thing he had ever seen had stopped on the roadside and men were getting out of it and coming down the bank, each carrying a box and a long, thin bag. They passed the squirrels' hiding place and, by moving to another porthole, Crag could see the men joining sticks together and settling down at the water's edge to dangle things that he could not quite see in the rising waters near the bridge.

Chip lay quietly on the floor savouring the same cared-for feeling from the fabric of the boat as he had sensed beneath the hut on the previous night. Crag hopped down from the seat.

"We must stay in here for a while," he said before he commenced the Morning Prayer, which was followed by a longer than usual period for contemplation of their sins. Chip was glad of the extra rest-time, though he tried not to let it show, just storing away the memory of his enjoyment of the cared-for feeling, to be purged by apologies to the Sun at the next prayer session.

Crag climbed back on to the seat and watched through the round window.

The sun had climbed high in the sky over Portland when the coach returned to pick up the fishermen, who joked and chaffed one another as they passed the boat on its trailer at the head of the little beach, before swinging themselves up into the vehicle.

As it pulled away, the squirrels, thinking that it was now safe to leave the boat, were about to squeeze under the cabin door when another travelling-box, squarer than most and with a cloth-covered back, came bumping down over the gravel track from the road. They did not move as the Land Rover backed up to the front of the trailer. Crag, watching awkwardly through one of the forward portholes, saw two humans leave the vehicle and come towards the boat. One went out of his sight, but he saw the other bend down and suddenly the angle of the boat's floor changed as the bow was lifted and the trailer was connected to the towing-hook. Crag dug his claws into the fabric of the seat and held tight, but Rusty and Chip were tumbled and thrown into a heap by the unexpected movement. They got up and dusted off their fur, and Chip looked apprehensively at his parents.

Rusty, seeing her son's concern, said, "The Sun must have this planned for us. I am sure that we will be safe." Then, turning to Crag, she asked, "Can we have the Danger Prayer?"

Crag, peering through the porthole, tried to keep his

balance while the boat rocked and tilted as the trailer carrying it was towed up the uneven bank and on to the road. He dug his claws into the fabric again and said in a loud voice,

We worthless squirrels,
Not understanding your plans
Crave your protection.

It is the Unknown
That we fear. In your good time
Please enlighten us.

The rocking stopped, and Crag saw the water of the lagoon pass below them as the Land Rover, with its boat-trailer in tow, crossed the bridge to the Mainland, then pulled up a hill with Man-dens on either side. The sensation was totally alien to him. Never in his entire life had he been *inside*, or even *on*, anything that moved in this way. He tried to establish what was reality. About him was the boat, apparently still, apart from a slight rocking motion, but, if he could believe his eyes, the world was moving past *him*.

He called to Rusty, who was crouched on the floor with Chip, "Come up here and look at this. Tell me what *you* see."

She hopped up on to the seat and Chip, risking his father's wrath, also hopped up, and the three of them each stared out through a porthole.

Man-dens and great trees were rushing past their eyes. One huge Man-den had a cliff of its own at the far end, soaring up into the sky. Seeing it, Chip felt a strong urge to be on familiar rock again, high up where he could observe his surroundings and the world was a stable place.

The passing trees created a different and less familiar urge in him, though equally strong. The soft-looking brown stuff that covered their trunks and branches attracted him. His claws itched, and he sensed instinctively that he would feel secure if he could only dig them deep into it.

The youngster waited for the inevitable order from his father to get down on to the floor. He must surely be noticed on the seat at any moment, he thought, but the order didn't come – Crag, with Rusty beside him, was staring out of the window as though mesmerised by the scenes rushing past.

Chip peeped out again. More Man-dens, more trees, green fields like those on the top of Portland, but with hedges and trees around them, then round-topped ridges – all passed in front of him. On one hillside was the gigantic figure of a human sitting on a horse, cut out of the browny-green of the turf and shining white in the September sunshine.

As they travelled on he began to enjoy himself; it was turning out to be a most exciting day. He knew, though, that he would have to repent for all this enjoyment later.

Then, with his brain a whirl of unaccustomed images, he noticed that the movement of the trees past the window was slowing, and he hopped down to the floor, to sit there demurely. Rusty followed him, but Crag stayed on the seat as the trailer was backed into the gaping doors of a barn. Here it was unhitched from the Land Rover and the floor resumed the angle that they recognised from the previous night. The humans went away and the barn doors were closed, leaving them in silence and semi-darkness. Chip suddenly felt frightened, hungry and sick. His punishment must be starting.

Crag's voice, lacking, for the first time that Chip could recall, that tone of total authority, said, "When it has been quiet for a while, we will go out and see why the Sun has tested us this way. But this is the Mainland and we must pray for guidance." He turned to Chip. "Then we must seek a worthy squirrel as your mate."

Chapter 5

Blood, a pine marten, was moving about in the darkness of his cage, fretting at the confinement and the stench in the dilapidated stable building near the isolated cottage on Middlebere Heath. He was forced to share this dark space with other animals who bore a resemblance to him in shape, though some were of a much smaller size.

A mature pine marten, or "sweetmart", to give him the Old English name, should be out amongst the trees in the forest, not shut up here, he was thinking.

From the cage below him another wave of noxious scent rose from the pair of "foulmarts", or polecats as they were more commonly called. He retched and tried again to find a way out.

The weasels and stoats were also moving about in their cages, equally uneasy; they had their own dreams of freedom and of a destiny dictated by their wits, instincts and survival ability.

Only the ferrets, born into captivity, were sleeping when the black door of the old stable was quietly opened. The human scent that blew in was not that of their gaoler, and the animals crouched, their hearts beating fast with anticipation. Two hooded humans entered, one, a male, carrying a set of bolt-cutters. The other, a female, stood watching at the door and shining the light from a tiny pencil-torch to guide her companion as he pulled out the pins or cut the padlocks securing the doors on each of the cages. Then, one by one, the cage doors were opened to allow the animals to leave. All, fearing these unknown humans, huddled in the back of their boxes until one of the ferrets, now awake and alert, ventured out on to the cobbled floor, saw an inviting trouser leg and, remembering the titbits that his human "master" had given him when they performed their joint party-trick, climbed up the leg inside. The ferret was not unduly put out to find that this human was not wearing the usual two pairs of trousers. He dug his claws in and scrambled up. The leg shook violently.

The man swore.

"Quiet!" hissed the human female.

"There's something climbing my leg. God, it's inside! Here, where's the light?"

"Quiet!"

"There's something in my trousers, I tell you. Oh my God! Shine that damn torch over here."

The man was attempting to take off his trousers whilst standing up, with his shoes still on his feet. The girl was flashing the light in his direction and trying desperately not to laugh.

In the confusion the pine marten, Blood, saw his chance and slipped away, out of the stable and into the fresh air outside. As he did so, the cottage door burst open; a human figure ran out and was momentarily silhouetted against the light behind. Blood saw that the man was holding a stick that was thicker at one end than the other, but knew that he was safe. He ran past the black hen-house, in which the disturbed chickens clucked fretfully, and into the night.

In the cool darkness there was the scent of resin and pine-bark. Blood padded on, heading northwards towards the long ridge of Arne, pausing now and then to sniff and to listen. He climbed the first tree to loom up ahead of him and lay on a branch, savouring his freedom.

When it was light enough, he looked about him. He was hungry and, more than anything else, he wanted *warm* flesh and blood, not the cold rabbits and dead chicken carcasses that had been his fare since his capture so far away in his northern homeland. He moved along the pine branch and leapt effortlessly into the next tree, then went on across the wood, pausing frequently to test the air and watch below him for possible food. An autumn-fat squirrel would be ideal, he thought, but there was not the slightest trace of squirrel-scent in the air or on the branches. He jumped from a pine into an oak tree.

A blackbird was rustling the leaf-litter below the oak and he stalked down the trunk, then pounced, catching the unwary bird whilst its beak and eyes were under the leaves. The pine marten scampered back up the tree, the limp bird in his mouth, enjoying the satisfying salty taste of warm blood. A trail of soft black feathers floated away on the morning air behind him.

Freedom and life for him, terror and death for others. Blood-dread had arrived!

Chapter 6

Across the waters of Poole Harbour, on the Island of Brownsea, enough red squirrels to satisfy even Blood's wildest dreams were planning to celebrate their Harvest. This island, known to the squirrels as Ourland, was an overgrown animal paradise of some five hundred acres of trees, heath and neglected fields, surrounded by a narrow beach.

Since the abdication of the last of the Royal squirrels the indigenous island community and the refugees from the Blue Pool Demesne had been integrating well. The islanders had adopted most of the refugees' customs and traditions, and many of them had accepted Tags awarded by Clover, who combined her Caring vocation with that of Tagger.

The ex-zervantz, now as free as any squirrels anywhere, were learning to live with the concept that they could make choices, and were getting used to the heady feeling of carrying their tails high and not always having to hold them in the submissive position.

Like the ex-Royals, the ex-zervantz still spoke with the 'z' dialect, but all were attending the sessions held to teach

OURLAND
BROWNSEA ISLAND

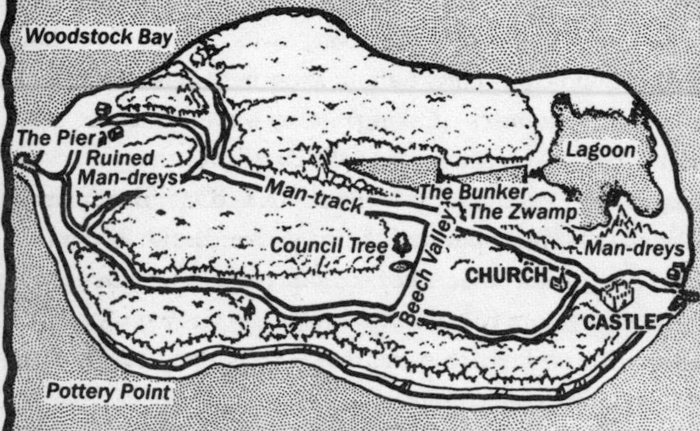

them the ancient Kernels of Truth which were replacing the discredited Royal Law.

Most of them had adopted new names, the males from trees and the females from flowers, but a few of the older ex-zervantz clung to their creepy-crawly names, amongst them Beetle, Bug and Caterpillar. These three old zervantz were the ones who had found it hardest to accept the changes, even though they enjoyed no longer being at the beck and call of each and any of the Royals. *That* way had always been their life, however, and whilst they had grumbled and complained about their treatment then, they now had difficulties making their own decisions and sometimes hankered for the "Old Days".

Much had changed for them, but Bug, Beetle and Caterpillar had maintained their "Zecret in the Zwamp".

Every autumn that they could remember they had slipped away from Royal duties and built a great mound of wet, dead leaves; in this steaming mass they had buried pawfuls of ripe sloes and left them there to ferment. During the following winter just eating one of these ruddled fruits was enough to make them forget all their troubles and cares, at least until the next morning, when they usually wished that they had left the sloes buried in the leaf-pile still.

On this autumn day Oak the Cautious, now Leader of the united Ourlanders, was at the Council Tree in Beech Valley near the centre of the island, talking to Fern the Fussy, his life-mate, and Clover the Tagger.

"We must have a Sun-day soon, to thank the Sun for allowing us to get the Harvest in. I think we've stored more reserves than ever this year," he said.

"I don't recall ever seeing so much food, and it is a beautiful island. The Sun certainly smiled on us when he guided us here," said Clover.

Fern looked to the west. "I wonder how Marguerite and the others have fared this autumn? At least we know that they're safe."

Oak followed her gaze. "I wonder if we will ever see our grand-dreylings. I suppose not. They could never find a way to come here. Remember all the luck we had on our journey here?"

"I like it on Ourland – it's so peaceful and safe, and food is so plentiful – but I *do* miss the Blue Pool. Couldn't we go to them?" said Fern.

Tansy the Wistful had just arrived and overheard the latter part of the conversation. "I'd find a way," she said confidently.

Clover smiled. Tansy had spent so much time looking out to sea after Marguerite and her party had been forced to leave that she had earned her Wistful tag.

"How would you get across the water?" she asked.

"I'd find a way," Tansy said again.

On the other side of the harbour Blood wandered along the shore, frustrated at the sight of the fat ducks who had just flown low over his head and landed in the shallows, and were paddling about out of his reach. Their scent wafted towards him on the easterly breeze, making his mouth water. He was quite ready to swim out to them, but knew that it would be a wasted effort as the ducks would be up and away long before he could reach them.

Then, faint but unmistakable, mixed in with the scent of

the ducks, was *squirrel-scent.* He stood up on his hind legs and tested it. Definitely squirrels – red squirrels. He sniffed again, then moved along the beach until he was clear of the duck-scent. Undoubtedly red squirrels, male *and* female, but a long way off, and over the water. Blood romped along the shore, looking for a way to cross the channel, then, realising that there was no landbridge, he slipped into the sea and swam across to the first of the islands.

There was no squirrel-scent here on Long Island and the breeze had dropped, so he spent the rest of the day quartering the island out of sheer curiosity, and searched along the shore until he found an injured seagull, unable to fly. He killed the weak bird easily, ate until he was full, glanced at the angle of the setting sun and decided that the squirrels would still be wherever they were tomorrow. He slept comfortably in a patch of reeds till dawn.

The morning breeze from the east carried the faint but tantalising scent, but the next land that Blood could see in that direction was a long way off.

He went to the south end of the island and swam across the channel to the Mainland, and waded ashore through the mud and rushes on a projecting point.

Time no longer mattered, discomfort was irrelevant, a swim was nothing; the squirrel-lust was on him. It took three days for him to reach Brownsea (by way of Green Island and Furzey Island), where, as he scrambled ashore, the air was thick with the scent of delicious squirrels. He padded up the bank behind the beach, through a stand of pine trees and on to a level grassy area, ignoring the rabbits which just looked up from their nibbling as he passed, showing no fear. Blood crossed an overgrown meadow and entered a wood, climbing into the trees to avoid the dense rhododendron bushes that covered the ground and moving upwind all the time.

It was in the swamp that he found a squirrel, asleep on the ground close to a pile of steaming leaves. In killing and eating it he both satisfied and inflamed the squirrel-lust burning inside him.

This place, he thought, is a sweetmart's dream. He searched for and found a perfect hiding place in a large, disused Man-cave, around which brambles and ivy grew, covering much of the stonework. After entering the arched entrance where the sun-bleached, wooden door stood ajar, he picked his way over the droppings from the huge and unknown birds he had seen outside, who clearly slept perched on the backs of the mouldering pews. At one end of the great cave he found a hanging rope, and climbed up it into the tower of St Mary's Church, Brownsea, there to sleep and dream of squirrels, and yet more squirrels.

Chapter 7

The Sun-day at the Blue Pool was nearly over. Well into autumn, the daily flood of human Visitors had ceased, and the squirrels had enjoyed a day of feasting, chasing and hiding. There had been a great deal of squirrelation, and now the tired and happy animals were making their way to the Council Tree to hear Dandelion tell one of the stories of Acorn, the first squirrel in the world. Squirrel-mates sat together and unmated youngsters sat with their friends, giggling and jostling for the best positions.

It was here that the Portland squirrels had found them, following the scent and the unfamiliar sounds of enjoyment that had drifted downwind towards the barn that afternoon.

Crag, Rusty and Chip had waited in the boat for an hour before cautiously emerging from their hiding place and dropping over the side on to the barn floor. Wriggling under the huge black wooden doors, they had blinked at the light, then clambered up the stone wall to where they felt safer, on the roof.

From there Chip had looked about him ecstatically. All

around him were trees, trees of every size and shape; their colours ranged from a light green to bright red, and the leaves had the strangest variety of patterns. The Mainland scents had made his head reel; the salty sea-smell of the Portland air was gone, and in its place was an atmosphere of moist leaves, resin and autumn fungus, underlaid by the warm hay-smell from bales stacked at one end of the barn beneath them. His nostrils had been assailed from every side and he had sniffed in pleasure and wonderment. Rusty was doing the same, though Crag was more soberly scenting around and analysing odours.

"There's a group of squirrels upwind," he had said, "probably a mile away. We'll go there and maybe make contact. There might be a worthy mate for you among them."

Chip had tried to hide his excitement, but a little trickle of urine had run down the roof-slates below him.

Crag had looked at him coldly. "Follow me," he had said, and they had followed him back down the barn wall, before crossing the grass and climbing an ash tree.

Chip had never known such a satisfying feeling in his life. Instead of searching the cold rock for a hold, everywhere that he put his paws his claws sank sweetly into the bark and it held him just where he wanted to be.

Crag had allowed them to practise climbing up and down the tree-trunk and running out along the branches.

This must be what my claws were really made for, Chip had thought, as he scratched at the bark and smelt the essence of the tree, moist under his paws.

Then it had been time to leap to the next tree. This was another new and thrilling experience – to leap across space with nothing beneath you and to land in a leafy, twiggy mass, full of paw holds, there to regain balance, before running along a thickening branch to the trunk of that tree.

"Don't get carried away. This isn't a game," Crag had warned him.

Chip had no idea what a game might be, but knew from the tone of his father's voice that the pleasure he had felt must be sinful and therefore hidden, and repented later.

The three had moved from tree to tree, travelling up the wind-line, the scent of strange squirrels getting stronger, until even Chip's unpractised nose could detect it.

They had then come to some pine trees surrounding a large pool, where they had paused, watching the blue of the water fading to green in the gathering dusk. Chip was thinking, sinfully, that he had never seen such a beautiful place in all his life.

They had heard the sound of excited squirrel chatter from the trees on the other side of the water.

"Follow me quietly," Crag had whispered. "Try not to show yourselves."

They had circled the pool and come to a large pine. Here they stopped and listened, concealed behind a screen of pine needles. Many other squirrels were sitting in the next tree, whilst others moved about from group to group.

Chip, quivering from head to foot, felt waves of the cared-for feeling radiating outwards from the assembled squirrels. What seemed to him to be the strangest thing of all was that they were touching each other as they sat. He felt a great urge to leap across and nestle in amongst them, but one look at his father's stern face killed that idea.

"Quiet," Crag said, keeping his voice low, and the three sat silently, watching and listening.

"Once upon a time," Dandelion started, in the traditional way of all story-tellers, after the squirrels had settled down to listen, "when the world was very young and there were only two squirrels in it – Acorn and his life-mate, the beautiful Primrose – the Sun looked down and saw that the ground was a mess. No animal or bird ever bothered to hide its droppings, and smelly piles were everywhere.

"In those days it rained only at night: just enough rain to water the plants and the trees and to keep the pools and rivers full, but not the heavy rain needed to wash all the muck away. So the days were always bright and sunny for the creatures to enjoy.

"The Sun let the animals and birds know that they must *bury* their droppings, so that the food they had once eaten could be used again by the plants, but all the creatures were too busy doing other things, and the world was so big it didn't matter. And if all the others buried theirs, it wouldn't matter about their own. All the reasons under the Sun why *others* should do it – but not them.

"Soon it got so that no animal could walk on the ground without treading in horrid things, so the Sun let it be known that if the world was not cleaned up, *something* would happen.

"Each animal and bird looked at the mess and said to itself, I only did a tiny part of that – others did most of it. So each did nothing and, as every creature thought exactly the same, the world stayed in a mess.

"Then one morning, when Acorn and Primrose woke up,

it was raining. They looked out of their drey and the rain was pouring down. This was so unusual that Acorn said the Asking Kernel:

Oh Great Loving Sun,
Please explain to us squirrels –
Why is it raining?

He couldn't add 'in the daytime', which is what he meant, because only five word-sounds are allowed in the last line, but the Sun understood, and made the water at the foot of his tree flash and sparkle so that Acorn could see *his* droppings tainting the pureness, and he was ashamed. It was too wet now to go down and bury them, so he went back into his drey and hid there with Primrose.

"Now, I forgot to tell you that Acorn and Primrose were then living in a sequoia tree on the top of a great rock called Portland, and *that* was the highest tree in the whole world."

Crag turned to Rusty and whispered, "This is all nonsense. Sequoia trees don't grow on Portland!"

Rusty and Chip, however, were listening intently to Dandelion, who continued. "After a few days, when it had never stopped raining, lots of animals waded or swam across from the Mainland to Portland, as they could see it was soon going to be the only part of the world above the water.

"Below where he sat in the sequoia, Acorn could see that some humans were building a boat, big enough to take them and lots of animals as well. By the time it was finished the sea was right up to the top of Portland and washing around the roots of Acorn and Primrose's home-tree. The man was asking all the animals and birds if they would like to come into his boat, and they were all going in and taking their mates with them. This was right at the beginning of the world, before any creatures had had any youngsters, so there were only two of each animal.

"The man called up to Acorn and Primrose and told them to hurry, but Primrose said to Acorn, 'I think that man eats animals. *I'm* staying here.' So the two squirrels stayed in their tree as the boat floated away on the flood.

"It rained and rained and rained, and the water came higher and higher up the tree, until Acorn and Primrose's drey was washed away. The two wet squirrels huddled together against the trunk, higher up, trying to keep dry, and then scratched out a little den in the deep, soft bark to shelter in.

"But the next day the water was up to that level, and they had to make another den-hole even higher. Each day the flood rose and rose, until the only bit of the tree above the water was the very tip-top twig. Acorn and Primrose clung to it, wondering what to do next.

"Acorn said the Needing Kernel:

Oh Great Loving Sun
What I need most at this time –
Is for the rain to stop.

But as this had six word-sounds instead of five, it kept on raining. Then Acorn tried again:

Oh Great Loving Sun
What I need most at this time –
Is for no more rain.

Since he had got the word-sounds right, the Sun drove

away the clouds and with them the rain, and soon the water started to go down and down.

"Primrose joined Acorn in saying the Thank You Kernel:

Oh Great Loving Sun
We, your grateful squirrels, now –
Thank you sincerely.

"Then, as the Sun shone to dry the wet squirrels, a great rainbow formed in the sky and, right in the middle of the arch, they could see the man's boat coming back towards them. Finally it grounded on the top of Portland where it was rising out of the water.

"Soon the animals were coming off the boat, two by two. First came two horses, then a cow and a bull, then two dogs, then two foxes, and two cats and all the other animals in pairs, except . . . there was only *one* unicorn, and that was looking sorrowfully and accusingly at the man as it came down the gangplank on to the soggy ground.

"The man shrugged his shoulders and held out his hands palms upwards. Primrose turned to Acorn and said, 'I told you so!'

"Now, you would think that all the creatures would have learned a lesson and buried their droppings after such an event, but they had soon forgotten what had happened, and behaved just as they had done before. So the Sun *still* has to send lots of rain to clean up the world.

"Today, only the cats and humans hide their droppings, and that is why cats hate the rain and humans are always grumbling about the weather."

Dandelion signalled that this was the end of the story and

her audience thanked her. After brushing whiskers with their friends, they set out for their own dreys in the near-darkness, the Sun-day over.

Crag whispered to Rusty and Chip to follow him, and the three slipped unnoticed away through the branches, Crag mumbling, "Blasphemy, blasphemy! It can't be true. *We* know that there are no sequoia trees on Portland. Blasphemy! Heathens, pleasure-seekers, every one of them!" Then, to Chip's disappointment, he added, "We won't find a worthy mate amongst that lot."

Chip was looking over his shoulder, hardly able to believe that there were so many other squirrels in the world and desperately wanting to stay and . . . and . . . Finding no words for "play with", "share with" or even "live with", he settled for wanting to just "be with" these warm and interesting animals that he felt so close to.

"Come on," his father called back gruffly. "There's nothing for you there."

Chapter 8

Blood woke from his dreams in the bell-tower of the disused church, shook himself and came tail first down the bell-rope and into the nave, wrinkling his nose in disgust as the stink of peafowl droppings filled his nostrils. The huge birds were roosting in rows along the back of the pews, and the sunlight, striking through the dusty stained-glass window, lit up the glossy blue of their necks.

Easy meat, thought Blood, but I can take those any time, and he slipped out through the door and down to the swamp to the place where he had found the ruddled squirrel on the previous day. There were no squirrels at the leaf-pile, but he played with the tail and the ragged skin of yesterday's meal, tossing it into the air and catching it, savouring the scent, until, filled again by squirrel-lust and hunger, he climbed a tree and set off on a hunting expedition.

Ex-Kingz-Mate Thizle had been visiting the drey of her son, once Prince Poplar, but who now insisted on being called Just Poplar, and was returning to her own drey through the treetops. She was disappointed yet again that he still showed no sign of being interested in finding a life-mate amongst the incomers' families. She was relieved, though, that he was not so taken by their classless ways that he might choose a female ex-zervant. That would be intolerable. She hoped that she had put a stop to any ideas he might just be having in that direction.

As he neared her drey, between the Zwamp and the Lagoon, she stopped and stared. A brown creature, larger than a squirrel, was climbing up the trunk of her drey-tree. She watched as it pushed its head into the drey and pulled out the Ex-King by the throat. She realised with horror that the creature could only be a pine marten. Terrified, she ran off to warn the other squirrels, finding most of them with Oak the Cautious, finalising the plans for their Harvest Sun-day.

"The King huz been killed and eaten," she gasped breathlessly, forgetting to use the "Ex". "There'z a pine marten on Ourland! A pine marten! Him'z killed and eaten the King!"

They all knew about pine martens, though only from stories and a silly Kernel that they told to unruly youngsters:

Pine marten's sharp teeth
Bite off the ears and the tails
Of naughty dreylings

The idea of a real-live pine marten being on Ourland was horrific. There weren't even dogs and foxes here!

"Are you sure?" asked Chestnut the Doubter.

"Uz zaw it eat the King. Him wuz much bigger than uz iz," she sobbed, "and the zame zort of colour but with white edgez to him'z earz and him can go up a tree az fazt az uz can. What'z uz going to do?"

The squirrels chattered in excitement and fear, looking round as though expecting hordes of bloodlusting pine martens to leap on them, until Oak, exerting his authority, said calmly, "We must hold a Council Meeting to discuss this. In the meantime we will set out watchers to warn us if it is coming this way."

Using the lessons learned the previous year, when they had had to defend themselves from a group of hostile grey squirrels on the Mainland, all those living in outlying dreys were encouraged to come and build nearer the Council Tree. Pickets were set to keep a constant watch.

Having temporarily satisfied his squirrel-lust, and finding that a peafowl would provide a meal for days, Blood stayed in the church, taking a roosting peahen occasionally and seldom venturing out.

The squirrels soon began to believe that the alarm must have been a product of Thizle's imagination, despite the disappearance of Ex-King Willow and the ex-zervant Bug, and relaxed their guard.

A week later the elderly ex-zervantz, Caterpillar and Beetle, drawn by an urge to get thoroughly ruddled again, sloped off unnoticed to the leaf-pile in the Zwamp.

Beetle ate first and was enjoying the drowsy, warm feelings when he saw Caterpillar, who had just dug himself a ruddled sloe from deep amongst the steaming leaves, staring past him. Fear was showing in his stance and in the look in his eyes. Beetle froze. Caterpillar started to move backwards, still with his eyes fixed on something behind

Beetle, whose neck-fur was now rising and his tail-tip swishing uncontrollably to left and right.

Beetle turned fearfully to look over his shoulder, caught a glimpse of sharp white teeth above a white-furred chest; he tried to leap for a tree, but fell in a heap as his limbs seemed to tangle with one another. Then he felt the teeth biting deep into his neck.

Caterpillar dropped the sloe he was holding without even a taste and, turning, abandoned his old ruddling friend to his fate and raced off through the trees to Beech Valley, where he described how Beetle had been killed in such vivid detail that even Chestnut could not doubt him.

There *was* a pine marten loose on their island!

Chapter 9

Next to be taken was a youngster, Hornbeam the Disobedient, who, living up to his tag, had wandered off in search of his favourite fungus and did not come back. His distraught mother pleaded for a search party to go and find him; four squirrels, led by Chestnut, set out cautiously, to return shortly with a limp red tail.

The Council was meeting twice a day trying to come up with ideas for defence, but no useful suggestions were forthcoming until Tansy the Wistful reminded the squirrels of the Woodstock, the magical vine-strangled stick with which her friend Marguerite had accidentally killed an aged Royal the previous year. Marguerite had had it with her when she left Ourland and it must surely be with her now at the Blue Pool.

"If we could get the Woodstock here, we could use it to kill the pine marten and we'd all be safe again," she said.

Her listeners chattered with relief. The Woodstock. Of course, why hadn't they thought of that?

Then reality returned. Some squirrel, or squirrels, would have to get to the Mainland, journey to the Blue Pool, collect the Woodstock – if it *was* in fact there and still worked – learn how to use it and get it back again to Ourland. The whole idea was impossible. They all sat in silence again, tails drooping with disappointment.

"Perhaps we could find another Woodstock on the beach," said Heather Treetops hopefully. Then, realising how unlikely this would be, she added, "Or perhaps we could make one. I sort of remember what it looked like."

Over the next two days, in the protection of watchful pickets, the squirrels looked for suitable fallen branches and pieces of driftwood. Using their teeth, they tried to re-create the twisted spiral they knew as a Woodstock. Some said that the twist ran one way and some said it ran the other, and several "Woodstocks" were made – but none had the smooth lines of the original or seemed to hold any feeling of hidden power.

"I think it was Marguerite's numbers that made it work," said Oak. "Does anyone remember how they looked?"

Her practice scratches on the sand had long since washed away, and the odd pieces of driftwood in which numbers had been cut by her teeth had floated off to other shores.

Clover recalled that Marguerite had cut numbers in the living bark of some birch trees, but these birches were too near the church where the marten's den was thought to be. Another Council Meeting was summoned, but no new ideas were forthcoming.

Tansy looked round at the despondent squirrels and thought of a Kernel taught to her by Old Burdock, the beloved and much respected elderly Tagger who had been such an inspiration to them on their journey to Ourland. Burdock had been Sun-gone since the summer and was buried in the ground below the Council Tree where they were now sitting.

The Kernel said:

If you think you can
Or if you think you cannot
Either way it's true

"I'll go and get the real Woodstock," she told them, and before any could object or raise difficulties, or try to convince her it was impossible, she leapt from the Council Tree and set off through the treetops towards Pottery Point, the nearest place on the island to the Mainland.

Watchful for the pine marten and surprised at her own boldness, Tansy jumped from tree to tree, wondering how she could ever cross the frightening stretch of water she could see ahead.

In a pine tree above the shore she stopped, plagued by doubts. The Sun had sent a door to carry them across to Ourland when they had been pursued by the Greys, and she half expected to see that very door drifting in on the tide. She stared out over the water, but could see nothing. What a fool she had been. Now she would have to go back and admit defeat. No she wouldn't.

Old Burdock had taught them when to use the Needing Kernel, having emphasised that it was for needing and not just for wanting.

Tansy looked up at the Sun and said the first part of the Kernel:

Oh Great Loving Sun
What I need most at this time
Is . . .

Her mind went blank as she struggled to find four more word-sounds to express her wish to cross the water.

A male sika deer, who had swum over to the island a moon before to serve the hinds there, stepped out of the bushes and paused below the tree in which Tansy sat, exhaustion showing in his eyes and stance.

A weary stag, she thought. Sun-inspired, she said aloud, "Is a weary stag", and dropped from the tree to cling to his left antler. The stag shook his head in irritation, gently at first, then violently, but Tansy held tightly to the hard horn. The stag waded into the sea and swam towards Furzey Island, tilting his head backwards and sideways as he swam, so that the water washed over Tansy, who clung there, terrified, salt water washing into her eyes, nose and mouth.

Just as she was thinking that she could hold on no longer, she felt the stag's feet touch bottom and he waded ashore on Furzey Island. Refreshed by the cold water and now seemingly unaware of the tiny sodden animal still clinging to his antler, he trotted across Furzey, entered the sea again and swam to the Goathorn Peninsula of the Mainland. As Tansy altered her grip, her foot touched the hair between the horns, and the stag tried to dislodge her by brushing his head against a bush. Tansy leapt into the foliage.

There *is* a way, she thought, if you think you can . . . She climbed a tree and licked herself dry, gagging at the taste of salt. Mentally and physically drained by her ordeal, she searched for and found an old magpies' nest in which to spend the night, alone for the first time in her life and fearful of every sound from the night-life all about her.

At dawn she set off through the plantation, keeping the sun behind her and heading in the direction that she hoped would lead to the Blue Pool, Marguerite and the Woodstock.

Chapter 10

On the night after their visit to the Blue Pool the Portlanders slept in a disused drey on the north side of the pool, well behind the screen of pine trees. The drey had been abandoned by grey squirrels when "Grades" – the Grey Death – had swept through there, wiping the colony out to a squirrel. The lingering scent of the Greys puzzled Crag. It was similar to red squirrel-scent, though subtly different. It was an unusual experience for him to be in a drey anyway, and the scent bothered him.

He had been tempted not to use the drey, which was, he thought, too comfortable for serious Sun-serving squirrels, but the temperature outside was falling fast and the stars were frost-bright above the trees.

"Just this once," he told Rusty and Chip. "Tomorrow we find a more appropriate place. We must get settled before winter really starts or we will starve or freeze to death."

Would he really care? Chip wondered. His father seemed to seek pain and discomfort. He would probably enjoy freezing to death, or starving.

Crag led the way into the moss-lined interior of the drey,

however, followed by Rusty and Chip, who was very conscious of the closeness of their bodies. There was no room to lie away from one another, and he lay awake, rigid and tense, next to his mother, feeling the warmth of her body against his own.

Later, much later, he dozed off, then woke to find his mother's paw around his shoulder and her tail covering him. He nestled against her and slept.

When he awoke at dawn, he found himself alone in the drey. He could hear his parents moving about outside.

"Don't let that youngster sleep on," Crag was saying. "Flush him out for prayers!"

Chip wriggled out into a world made magic by frost. Every twig and leaf was encrusted with crystals of ice, built from the mist that had drifted in over the land during the night and was now dissipating in the sunshine. Each crystal caught the light and sparkled in a tiny rainbow of colour. The young squirrel looked about him in wonder. It was all so beautiful.

"*Your* turn to say the Morning Prayer," said Crag.

Chip had done so several times before, using the standard wording as his father and mother had always done, but today, after the first section,

Be not too wrathful
Oh Great Sun, on those squirrels –
Who sinned in the night,

he felt moved to use his own words:

Thank you, oh Great Sun,
For the beauty of your light
In this sparkling world.

Rusty, thrilled by this unexpected prayer, turned admiringly towards her son, only to cringe as Crag reached out a paw and struck Chip across the head. "Blasphemer!" he hissed, and finished the prayer himself:

Let us serve your needs
For the whole of this your day
Weak though we may be.

Then, glowering at the unhappy youngster, he led his family down to forage on the chill ground. Later they would search for a permanent base to create a New Temple.

It was High Sun when Crag found what he was seeking. In a clearing in the wood a huge gnarled oak stood, twisted by age. Although it was blackened by fire from a lightning strike many years before, lingering autumn-brown leaves on a few branches indicated that it was not yet completely dead. A little way up the tree the hollow of the trunk forked to form two chambers above the large one below.

Crag explored all the hollows, then came down to where Rusty and Chip sat silently waiting on the ground.

"This will be our New Temple," he announced. "There are suitably austere sleeping places for each of us to have their own, and great chambers to store the metal collection."

Chip groaned to himself, his teeth hurting at the very thought of holding rusty things again. He looked appealingly at his mother.

"Is it wise to use a tree that has been struck by lightning? Might it not happen again?" she asked.

"Lightning never strikes twice in the same place," Crag assured her confidently. "Now we start the collection. Honour be to the Sun."

Chapter 11

Slate, a mature female grey squirrel, looked at the remains of the Oval Drey in the giant oak at Woburn Park. A winter and a summer of neglect had made the drey look unkempt and drab. It was hard to picture it as she had last seen it, bustling with activity. That was before the Grey Death had killed its inhabitant, the Great Lord Silver, as well as most of the other Greys in New America.

A few survivors were now clustered round, the males discussing what they should do to set up a centre of government again. Slate could see that they were all at least a year younger than she was and were obviously inexperienced.

"I would suggesst . . ." Slate began, the words hissing past her broken tooth.

As one, the males glowered at her.

"This is a formal meeting," a male – Basalt – said firmly. "Females may only speak when requested to report. You should know that."

"I jusst thought that sinsse so many thingss had changed . . ."

"Females shouldn't think," said Basalt, and turned away.

Slate sat on the branch, angry and frustrated. She had hoped that the one good thing to come out of the Grey Death tragedy might have been an opportunity to right some of the past injustices. Oh well, she thought, there are more ways of opening a nut than waiting for it to grow.

She listened in silence as the males continued. Basalt was dominating the conversation, talking down any opposition to his ideas.

"The Red Ones lived here long before our kind came from our homeland beyond the sunset. The Grey Death did not affect them, whereas it virtually wiped us out. Perhaps the way they live is the right way; here in New America at least."

"They're all squimps," said Chalk, unconsciously using a red word that had crept into their language. "They're all soft and gentle."

"So they may be," retorted Basalt, "but they are also alive. Those we haven't killed, that is. I think we should learn their ways.'

Slate was itching to intervene, but was not going to risk another public rebuff.

"Will we have a Great Lord Silver?" a male asked. "The Reds don't."

"Well, we don't have to do *exactly* what they do," said Basalt. "But we do need a leader to be in charge here and to direct other Greys who may have survived and come back to Base for guidance. The Reds would *choose* one, not fight for the position as we have always done. I propose that I am chosen as Great Lord Silver. All agree? Right. That's settled, then."

The Greys looked at one another in amazement, but Basalt continued quickly, "Who knows anything about the customs of the Reds?"

"They have different names from us," said Chalk. "The males are named after trees and the females after flowers."

"We'll start there, then," said Basalt. "Each squirrel is to choose a new name, but choose trees and flowers from the Old Country."

"I'll be Hickory," said Chalk.

"Sitka for me," said Shale. "I never did like my name anyway. Basalt, you should be Redwood, if you want us to do what a Red would."

This pun, the ultimate form of grey humour, was received with groans. Basalt agreed rather than argue with another squirrel who had just chosen Tamarack, a name he had intended to use himself. He'd got away with appointing himself Great Lord Silver and was not going to push his luck further.

The females had grouped together and were discussing names for themselves. One chose Prairie Rose, another Yucca, and, amid laughter, Tufa turned down a proposal that she be called Skunk Cabbage in favour of Bluegrass.

"What about you?" Yucca asked Slate.

"If we have to go along with thiss nonssensse, I want to be called Ivy," she replied.

"Poison Ivy?"

"Suitss me," said Ivy. "Lotss of true wordss are said ass jokess."

They rejoined the males. Redwood was now issuing orders.

"Hickory, I want you and Sitka to take a mixed party down to the Blue Pool in that part of New America that the Reds call Purbeck. It is the last place that I know of where Reds are definitely still living. Make contact with them and learn their ways. Don't argue, just do what they do. When we know all their habits and customs, we can modify them to suit ourselves."

"What if they fight us?" Sitka asked.

"Reds don't fight, they pray to the Sun. I told you, they are squimps," Hickory replied.

"Don't fight them; don't argue with them. Apologise for our past behaviour so that they are not suspicious. Learn their ways. That's an order." Redwood scowled at the squirrel before him.

"Yes, sir," said Hickory, saluting with his right paw held diagonally across his chest. "Trust me. We'll rest up and leave at first light."

"You'll leave now," said Redwood firmly. "If more Greys come in, I'll send them to join you. Listen and learn."

"Yes, sir," said Hickory, and saluted again.

Hickory had called a halt. He had been urging his group on at quite a pace. They had passed the ancient wood that the Reds had so stupidly called the New Forest, and were on the edge of the heathland that was reported to be the last barrier before the Blue Pool. It was there that the red survivors of the Greys' massacres were believed to be living.

The nights were getting much colder and they had to huddle together for warmth when they rested. Though it was now only mid-afternoon, he could sense that a chilly night was coming.

He looked at the other squirrels. They were in fair condition; dishevelled from their journeying, but in good spirits. Even Poison Ivy, notably older than the rest, was looking fit, if a little tired. She had been most useful in instructing him on the route, even though she had never come this far south or west before. She knew some of the Reds' Kernels of Truth, but she would never tell where she had learned them. How did they go? Five sounds, seven sounds, then five again; or was it six?

Hickory called Ivy over to join him. "How far do you think it is to that pool now?" he asked.

"Over the heather and beyond the treess," she answered enigmatically. "Send out some scoutss. The resst of uss can wait here. We will be safe in thosse piness."

Sitka and three other scouts left and, while they were away, a new group of Greys joined those waiting in the pine trees. Their leader explained that more and more survivors of the Grey Death were arriving at Woburn and many were being sent down to join Hickory's party in Purbeck.

"Redwood calls us all the Second Wave," he said proudly. "The Silver Tide was swept away by the Grey Death, but we are not to give up trying. The Second Wave *will* succeed. Praise to the Great Lord Silver."

What would they call a female Great Lord? Ivy was wondering.

The scouting party returned at nightfall with a report that they had scented Reds, but had not made contact. "Yes, there is a pool set in a hollow in the pine trees. Yes, it is blue. Move over, we're freezing. We're the ones who've been doing all the running round while you just sat about. Who are all you lot?"

"Be quiet and sleep," Hickory growled. "We leave before dawn. We should be with those Reds by sun-up."

Ivy looked forward to meeting them. She had heard that females were treated equally by the natives.

Chapter 12

Marguerite the Tagger woke on that frosty morning after the Blue Pool community's Harvest Celebrations and looked out from her drey. "Juniper," she called, "Oak, Burdock, come and see this", and her life-mate and their two youngsters emerged, looked around, then started to romp through the sparkling treetops, dislodging showers of ice-crystals which filtered down through the branches, catching the sunlight as they fell.

The squirrels' breath made white mist in the cool air as they leapt from tree to tree, their excitement spreading to other dreys until the trees of Steepbank seemed full of happy squirrels, all leaping and sporting in the shimmering treetops.

Then Marguerite noticed the grey squirrels below them. She counted. 1 2 3 4 5 6 7 — 10 11 12 13 14 15 16 17

"Oh, Sunless Pit," she sighed. "I thought we had seen the last of you!"

The Reds' excitement died as others followed her gaze. All the older Reds knew of the strife and trouble caused by the grey colonisers, and how squirrels like these had forced the natives to leave the Blue Pool for sanctuary on Ourland. There the surrounding sea had kept the Silver Tide at bay until the Grey Death swept it away.

One of the grey males hopped forward.

"We come in peace," he called up, keeping his tail in the submissive position. "We would like to talk."

"Stay on the ground," Marguerite called down, and, with Alder the Leader by her side, she dropped to a lower branch.

Alder left the talking to the Tagger, who, though female and younger than he, was a squirrel of "infinite resource and sagacity", as he was fond of describing her to others.

"What do you want of us?" she asked, remembering the territorial demands of the previous colonisers.

Their leader introduced himself. "I am Hickory and this is my second-in-command, Sitka. We are squirrels of the Second Wave and have come to live in peace with you."

Marguerite glanced at Alder. This was unexpected!

The Grey went on, "We have instructions from the new leader at Woburn to learn local customs and to live by those. Our leader has recognised that we were wrong in trying to impose *our* culture in another land.

"On behalf of all squirrels of our kind, I apologise for any sufferings the Silver Tide caused you. We have been punished with the scourge of the Grey Death and we are here to make amends."

"Fine words," Marguerite called down suspiciously. "How do we know that you mean them – and that this isn't a trick?"

"We have composed what you call a Kernel:

When in others' lands
Learn all the local customs,
Do as the Red Ones do."

Marguerite flinched at the extra word-sound in the last line. Not a true Kernel, she thought, but the meaning is good. She glanced again at Alder for authority to continue. He nodded and moved the stump of his tail in what would have been a flick of confirmation, had his tail not been severed after a clash with animals similar to those below them.

"We have suffered badly from squirrels like you, and are not yet ready to trust your intentions. There is vacant land to the north-east. You will know it by a great tree that has been struck by lightning. Spend the winter there, do not encroach, and in the spring, if we have come to trust you, we will meet again and teach you our ways."

The Greys raised and lowered their tails as a sign of acceptance, then meekly trooped away through the pines to find the Lightning Tree in the North-east Wood. The last to leave was Ivy, who was looking over her shoulder at the red female, but she had turned away.

"Well," said Marguerite after they had left, "what do we make of that?"

"I think you did the right thing," Alder told her. "They seemed contrite and well-meaning, but do animals like that really change their natures, just because of – what did they call it? – 'instructions from the new leader at Woburn'? I don't trust them." He reached back and rubbed the stump of his tail ruefully.

It's true, Ivy was thinking, that female was treated as an

equal. There were no fleas on her, though. Not one to be easily bettered in an argument. She might just be useful one day.

A few miles away to the east, between the Blue Pool and the shore of Poole Harbour, Tansy was losing some of her confidence. The Mainland now seemed very big and she was lonely. Having grown up in a community where the Council decided all major issues, she was not used to making many decisions on her own and found herself spending hours dithering whenever there was a choice of routes. She would choose one and start along it, only to change her mind, backtrack and take the other way. She wondered now how she had been so confident on Ourland.

Then, remembering the importance of her mission, she would press doggedly on. She *had* to find Marguerite and the Woodstock to save her family and friends.

Supposing she ran into any grey squirrels? But Marguerite's last message had said that they were all gone. She sniffed at the wind coming from the west. Could that be Greys' scent? It was faint if it was, but it certainly smelt like it. She trembled but pressed on.

Tansy was hungry and tired when she came to a Man-drey, outside which chickens pecked at grains of wheat and maize on the ground. A goose in the next field honked a warning as she approached, snaking her long neck through the wire at the squirrel and hissing ominously, but Tansy could see that the great bird could not get through the fence to harm her. She joined the chickens, enjoying the unfamiliar mealy taste of the dry yellow seeds, then, suddenly sensing the presence of a human dangerously near, turned to leap away.

She was too late to avoid the man's long-handled net.

Chapter 13

Crag dragged a rusted bolt to the Temple in the Lightning Tree. He had found the remains of an old wooden haywain and had set Rusty and Chip to gnaw at the partially rotted timbers in order to free the bolts. He carried them, one by one, up inside the Temple and placed them in nooks and crannies of the hollow branches, along with nails, screws and old cartridge cases that he had sniffed out in the undergrowth.

Coming back down the tree he stopped, peered below and rubbed his eyes. Clustered about the base of the trunk was a group of squirrel-like creatures with silvery-grey fur, looking up at him expectantly.

"Greetings to you, sir," one of them called up "Your friends at the Blue Pool sent us over here, but did not tell us that any other squirrel would meet us. I am named Hickory, and this is my second-in-command, Sitka. And your name, sir?"

"You are squirrels?" Crag asked.

"Why, yes, we thought all of the red kind knew about us by now. Had you not heard?"

"No! Until recently my family lived in isolation and we have only just come to the Mainland. Who are you?"

Crag came down to the ground and stood in front of the Greys.

"We are silver squirrels from over the sea to the west," Hickory told him. "Our ancestors were brought to this country, which we call New America, by humans and we have been setting up colonies here. Unfortunately, *some* silver squirrels got over-zealous and upset you natives. Then we suffered from a plague we called the Grey Death. Now our instructions are to work alongside you all and to learn your ways. So here we are!" He spread his paws wide.

"Did you say that you were sent here by the squirrels over at the pool?" Crag asked.

"Yes. They said we were to spend the winter here, but did not tell us that you would meet us. They were polite to us, but understandably suspicious. Well, here we are, sir." He waited expectantly.

Crag surveyed the Greys. They looked big and powerful, and had strong teeth.

"Follow me," he said, and led them off in the direction of the derelict haywain.

Tansy crouched in the corner of the dark cage. It was daytime, for she could see the winter light under the door, but it was too dark for her to make much sense of her surroundings.

The day before her captor's leather-gloved hand had taken her from the net and thrust her into the empty cage that had last been occupied by the pine marten. It was impregnated with his terrifying scent, but even this was submerged by the rank odours rising from the only other occupants of the cages, a pair of ferrets who snuffled and prowled about or slept noisily somewhere below her.

Tansy was still shaking with fright and her mind was going round in circles. She must get out to find Marguerite and the Woodstock to save the Ourlanders from the pine marten, but before she could do that she must get out to find . . .

The stable door opened and cold air rushed in. A man's dark eyes peered through the wire at her as he bent down to look into the cage.

"Come on, my lovely," he said, the words meaningless to Tansy. "I've brought you some special food."

In his hand was a paper bag containing a variety of Christmas nuts bought from a stall in Wareham market. He opened the cage door slightly and tossed in a handful, then closed it quickly. Tansy hid her head under her paws until he had gone out of the stable, leaving her once again in the cold darkness.

The nuts smelt strange and foreign; she felt for them in the sawdust of her cage floor and was puzzled by the waxy feel of the shells. The hazelnuts she knew, and the walnuts, but the strange three-cornered ones were new to her. She gnawed at the end of one until she could taste the oily kernel inside. She ate only a little of it, then opened a walnut, the flavour immediately bringing back memories of the celebration of the passing of the Longest Night, and the feasting the squirrels enjoyed when they knew the Sun would soon return with the warmth of spring.

Her spirits lifted by the man's gift, she tried every side of the cage for a way out, then crouched in a corner and recited to herself the Kernel of Encouragement:

When all is darkness
Squirrels need not fear for long,
The Sun will come soon

She searched again for a way to escape.

Blood was getting restless. He had finished eating the peahen that he had most recently killed in the church, had played with the feathers, slept for a full day and night and had then wakened with the squirrel-lust on him. He came down the bell-rope, passed the rows of dozing birds on the pew-backs and padded out into a grey winter day. He sprang up on to the gravestone of an earlier, human, inhabitant of the island and peered about, sniffing. The air was clear of squirrel-scent, so he made off towards the leaf-pile in the swamp. All hunters hope to find new quarry where they have successfully killed before.

Only the tails of his two previous victims were there. He sniffed at these until his mouth watered and his mind was filled with nothing but the urge to taste the blood of a squirrel. He ran up the trunk of an aspen tree and started his search.

Blood picked up recent squirrel-signs in Beech Valley. There were newly gnawed cones under the pine trees, fresh scratch-marks on the beech trunks and the tantalising smell was everywhere.

The pickets, though, had seen him coming and quickly spread the word. The females, the youngsters and the older squirrels had hurried off towards Woodstock Bay, whilst the fit males had watched Blood's movements from a safe distance. Soon they put their plan into operation. One, Just

Poplar, showed himself and tempted Blood to follow as he led him from tree to tree up the valley, keeping just far enough ahead of the pine marten to be safe, but near enough to keep Blood bounding through the branches at his fastest rate. Just Poplar knew that neither of them could keep up this pace and this knowledge was part of the Plan.

When he tired, he slipped behind a tree-trunk and the role of "tempter" was taken over by one of the ex-zervantz, Maple, previously called Maggot.

Maple was strong, fit and fresh, and set a merry pace to keep the marten from realising that he had been duped. The Plan was progressing well, the chase curving round and back towards the church. Even the last leap had been judged to perfection: Maple sailed over the gap between two trees that he had estimated was too wide for the heavier marten.

Blood, angry and breathing hard, glared after the departing high-tailed squirrel, gave up the chase, came down the trunk, went into the church and slaughtered a peahen. It was tame stuff, this, the stupid bird putting up little resistance as his teeth bit deeply through the feathers of her neck, the squawk of protest cut off in mid-call.

He ate his fill amongst the drifting specks of down, then climbed wearily up the rope to the bell-tower to sleep the remainder of the day away. Those squirrels would not catch him out with *that* trick again, he vowed to himself.

Ivy did not like the regime that Crag had imposed or the feeble way in which Hickory and Sitka accepted it. They might have instructions to learn the strange customs of the natives, but this metal collecting was a bore. Hickory and

Sitka seemed ready enough to carry out the instructions of the Temple Master, but whenever she had the chance, she would slip away from the work party and go off on her own. Sometimes she would go across to the Blue Pool and watch the Reds there, unobserved, from a distance, just to confirm that the one who called herself Marguerite was treated as an equal by the red males; it was clear that Crag had nothing but contempt for Rusty, his mate. Whenever she watched, she could see that Marguerite was not merely treated as an equal but held in very high regard.

Ivy had found a thin flat piece of grey stone near the haywain which, when she scratched it with another stone, bore a mark. One day, after deserting the working party, she went to where she had hidden this slate and drew the only marks that she could remember on it – 1 for one, 10 for two, 11 for three and 100 for four. This was how the Greys had counted before the Grey Death came, and she realised with a start that she was now probably the only Grey who remembered these marks and this way of counting. The idea troubled her. If she had died, all the knowledge of numbering would have died with her. She knew so much more about so many other things as well. There ought to be a way to record everything she knew, but how?

She wiped the slate clean and did a random line – 01000001.* She was looking at the shapes, her head tilted to one side, sensing some hidden meaning in these, when she heard a sound behind her and turned to face Marguerite.

* ASCII code for A.

Ivy was surprised to see how small this Red appeared against herself now that they were together on the ground. She did not feel in any way threatened.

"Hello," she said "I'm Ivy."

"I'm Marguerite the Tagger. I came to observe your party and found you on your own. What are you doing?"

Ivy's tail rose. She was flattered to find a senior squirrel interested in her scratching.

"We count thiss way," she said, drawing 1 10 11 and 100 on the piece of slate again. "But I have jusst drawn 01000001 and it seemss to be telling me something."

Marguerite looked hard at the figures. They were similar to the patterns made with twigs and fircones that the first Greys she had met used to make their numbers. Here was a special Grey that she might learn from. Numbers of any kind had always fascinated her.

"Marguerite!"

She looked up, startled at the savagery in Juniper's voice.

He was crouched on a branch above her, quivering with rage.

"Come up here at once. Now!"

Marguerite bristled with anger, yet dared not show disrespect to her life-mate in front of this stranger. She could appreciate Juniper's concern; his first life-mate, Bluebell, had been killed by Greys near that very spot only a year or so earlier.

She leapt for the tree-trunk as the Grey turned away.

Ivy left quickly, abandoning the piece of slate. So much for equality, she was thinking.

*

Hickory and Sitka were discussing Crag in a hollow on the ground near the Temple Tree.

"Do you think that Crag's got all his conkers?" Hickory asked.

"It's hard to tell," Sitka replied. "Apart from the Reds we saw over by the pool, and his mate and son, they're the only ones we've met. We were told that the natives have funny habits."

"I think I preferred the old ways – our parents would just have zapped the lot of them. Start clean, then. None of this Sunless Pit business and sleeping on your own."

"I don't like the sound of the Sunless Pit, so I'm not taking any chances. I'm going to keep my nose clean and my tail dry. Go along with what the old fellow says, for a while at least. Have you seen Ivy? She keeps sneaking away."

Sitka looked around. "We'd better be getting back ourselves, or old Tin Can will be after our tails!"

Chapter 14

Chip's days were fuller than ever before. His father kept him and his mother at full stretch, working alongside the funny grey squirrels, who were so polite to both his parents and himself. Crag had found a pile of assorted scrap metal behind an old Man-cave and had organised the full resources of his new team to carry out the task of moving all the smaller pieces up into the hollow trunk of the Temple Tree.

The Greys were now sleeping there too, every squirrel in a separate corner or bay of the hollows. Crag did the rounds at least once every night to make sure that each squirrel, of whatever colour, was sleeping alone, and not indulging itself with the warmth of a tail for cover.

Once, when it was particularly cold and Crag had just done his rounds, Young Chip, shivering and fearing a rebuff, had crept silently to where his mother was sleeping and had crawled in beside her. Although she must have known he was there, she said nothing and the two lay there through the bitter night, sharing each other's warmth and jointly fearing the Sunless Pit until, at the first glimmer of light, Chip crept away to his own corner, past the Greys that he could see were all religiously observing the "no tail warmth" edict.

At prayers, when Crag came to the "sinned in the night" part, Chip glanced at Rusty, but her head was, like her tail, meekly lowered.

Whenever he had the chance, Chip questioned the Greys about their lives and their beliefs, but they had little to say except that they were now contrite and sorry for what their kind had done to the Reds, and had instructions to learn and to live by the local customs, which would have evolved to suit the conditions in each locality.

On one such occasion Crag had come up behind him when Chip had paused in sorting metal and was talking to Hickory.

"Why do you call this country New America?" he had asked, then had reeled across the scrap-pile as his father had struck him a blow across his head.

Crag snarled, "Don't delay the work with useless questions. We, and that includes you, have a Temple to furbish. Fear the Sunless Pit!"

Chip, his head spinning, had gripped a piece from a broken ploughshare with his teeth and started to pull it backwards through the grass under the trees, in the direction of the Temple Tree.

Crag was thinking about his wonderful Temple. It was far better than the one in the cave on Portland, and the Sun had provided a team of workers to help him fill it with the precious metal. Chip's mating could safely be left until the next year.

By then the Temple would be full. The Sun could clearly

see that he, Crag, was a worthy squirrel and would direct them to find a worthy female as a suitable mate for his son. Not one of those Blasphemers over at the pool, with their false stories and immoral ways. He must make sure that Chip was worthy himself by then; he was a bit of a slacker at present.

Wood Anemone the Able and Spindle the Helpful, the ex-zervantz who had left Ourland with Marguerite, had settled well as free squirrels at the Blue Pool. Unlike the other Reds, they had no personal knowledge of how the natives had been treated by the Silver Tide and often spoke between themselves about the Greys.

They did not know of the incident involving Ivy, Marguerite and Juniper, nor about Marguerite's anger with her life-mate. Marguerite had been all for going over to the North-east Wood to apologise to Ivy,, but had been dissuaded.

"We agreed to leave them until after the winter. Then we will make formal contact," Juniper had told her, and since it had been a purely family matter, the Council had not been informed.

"Let'z go and zee what the Grey Wonz iz doing," Spindle suggested one afternoon.

"Do yew think uz zhould?" asked Wood Anemone.

"Well, there'z no taboo on it, and uz'z zurprised that Marguerite juzd zent them off like that lazd autumn. If they'z doing anything odd, uz could report back."

Their youngsters were away somewhere having fun of their own as Wood Anemone and Spindle left for the North-east wood. The slight feeling of unease that Spindle felt he put down to his years of being a zervant. Now he was free, he told himself, he could do as he wished, within the Kernel Lore, and there were no Kernels that he knew about not looking at Greys.

They reached the Temple Tree clearing and watched from behind a tree-trunk as the Greys carried various pieces of metal along the paths that converged there. They were wondering what it all meant when a native voice in an unfamiliar accent addressed them from behind. "An inspiring sight, is it not?"

They jumped and turned to face an unknown Red.

"I am Crag, the Temple Master," he said.

"Greetingz, Crag the Temple Mazder," said Spindle, wondering what a Temple was. "Uz iz Zpindle the Helpful and thiz'z uz life-mate, Wood Anemone the Able. Uz'z puzzled by what the Grey furred zquirrelz iz doing."

"They prefer to be called Silvers," Crag told him. "Are you from the Blasphem – the community at the pool?"

"Uz iz. Uz'z the Guardianz of Beachend, in the Blue Pool Demezne," Spindle told him proudly.

"That's a fine place," Crag responded. "Did you have a good Harvest?"

"Yez, zuperb," Wood Anemone told him. "Uz ztored lotz of nutz, enough to zee uz all right through the worzt winter – and the zpring!"

"I'm pleased for you," Crag told them. "Are you Sun-worthy?

"Zun-worthy?" Spindle looked at Wood Anemone and then back at Crag. "If yew meanz, do uz leave the eighth nut az the zun-tithe – yez, uz iz."

"No, I mean, do you worship the Sun?"

"Zurely the Zun doezn't need uz to worzhip it," said Spindle. "Uz would have thought it wuz above all that! Yew makez it zound like won of the kingz uz uzed to have on Ourland."

"Oh, no. The Sun needs worship, and metal to be brought to the Temple. And repentance for your sins!"

"What'z zynz?" Wood Anemone asked.

"Things you do to indulge yourselves – unworthy things," Crag told her.

Wood Anemone's face showed her lack of understanding, but she and Spindle waited for instructions. Crag's voice carried that tone of authority that commanded instant obedience and unquestioning acceptance. It was the voice that the Royals had always used. The two ex-zervantz waited in silence for Crag to continue – if he chose to do so.

Crag noted their tail-down attitude.

"In the name of the Sun, I command you to report the position and amounts of all your community's food reserves," he demanded, and unhesitatingly Spindle the Helpful, one-time zervant to the King of Ourland, gave the information.

"There iz many lotz of hazelnutz in the copze near the Dogleg Field. There iz lotz of chezdnutz . . ." He reported as he had done to the Royals on Ourland.

Crag listened intently.

When Spindle had finished, he said, "In the name of the Sun, I forbid you to tell any squirrel what you have seen today, or I, Crag the Temple Master, will ensure that it is the Sunless Pit for you, for your dreylings and for your dreylings' dreylings – for ever!"

"Iz there really a Zunlezz Pit?" Wood Anemone ventured to ask the stern, high-tailed Red.

"Oh, yes – it is an awful place where any blasphemers, and those who disobey a Temple Master, will exist in darkness for ever. Say nothing of our meeting or of what you have seen."

Spindle and Wood Anemone left the North-east Wood, their tails low, feeling that they had done something wrong, but they could not speak of it, even to one another.

Crag watched them go. He was memorising each hiding place. "Many lots of hazelnuts in the copse near the Dogleg Field, lots of chestnuts . . ."

Tansy had finished the nuts that she had been given and was hoping for more. Several times a day she searched for a way of escape, but each attempt was as fruitless as before.

Afraid of getting muscle-weak from inactivity, she would race around the netting of the cage until breathless, then crouch in the darkness, listening to the grumblings of the ferrets in their indecipherable "weasel" language.

She often recited the Kernel of Encouragement to herself, confident in her faith that the Sun would indeed come soon. Then she tried to recall other Kernels of Truth that she had been taught.

Some were routine, just instructions on drey-building, general cleanliness and what food was safe and what was not, but as she remembered each one, with plenty of time to think about it, she realised that most Kernels had much deeper, hidden meanings and that within them they contained a complete philosophy appropriate to the whole squirrel race. There was one that she especially liked, it seemed so apt now:

"Fear" sniffed at the drey,
"Courage" awoke and looked out –
But "Nothing" was there.

Tansy was saying this for the seventh time that day, savouring its message, when the door opened and the man came in holding the bag of nuts. Instead of staying at the back of the cage, Tansy came forward boldly and, as the lonely man opened the cage door and held out a Christmas walnut, "Courage" hopped on to his sleeve, ran up his arm and, from his shoulder, leapt for the daylight and freedom.

She scampered across the yard, past the man's Christmas dinner, which was hanging by its feet from an elder tree, scarlet blood pouring from its recently cut throat, and over the wall towards the first tree she could see. She climbed into a fork and looked back. The man had come out of the stable and gone across to the goose hanging from the elder tree. She watched him swing it violently to and fro, blood splattering across the ground and up the stone wall, before he went into the house.

Greys held no terrors for her now and, when she was sure that the man was not coming out to follow her, she headed directly for where she thought the Blue Pool to be, keeping to the trees wherever possible, but running openly along the ground when they were too far apart.

She spent one night in a hollow willow stump and another in a rabbit hole that was disused and damp. Finally, on a bitter winter day, with the east wind blowing her tail over her ears, she crossed the smelly Man-track and the railway, until only the North-east Wood stood between her and the Blue Pool.

In that cold, dank wood she smelt the oddly mingled scents of both Greys and unknown Reds. Then, along the path, came a first-year Red dragging a tangle of rusting wire.

She called to him and he looked fearfully over his shoulder before answering. He was tired and thin, and did not have the sleek, fat look that a well-fed midwinter squirrel should. Tansy, realising that she herself would not be looking at her best and might have frightened him with her sudden appearance, spoke to him formally.

"Greetings. I am Tansy the Wistful, on my way to the Blue Pool."

"Hello," said the young male, shyly.

Tansy waited for the formal response. When it was not forthcoming, she said, "Are you alone?"

"At the moment, yes. My mother is at the Temple and my father is with the Greys at the metal-pile."

"Is he safe with the Greys?" Tansy asked, and Chip looked puzzled.

"Oh, yes," he assured her. "They are cooperative."

Contrary to custom, Tansy had to ask his name.

"It's Chip," he told her, and she waited for the tag which would give her valuable clues as to the kind of squirrel he was. It did not come.

"Your tag?" She raised an inquisitive eyebrow and her tail indicated "question".

"I don't understand," Chip replied, looking worried.

A snowflake fell from the pink-grey sky and rested lightly on his whiskers. He brushed it away and looked up.

Suddenly the air was full of swirling, drifting flakes and the young male looked at Tansy in puzzlement, as though she were responsible for the phenomenon.

"What is this?" he asked.

"Snow," she replied. "We must seek shelter immediately."

"What about the metal?" Chip asked, indicating the baling wire.

"Leave that," she told him. "Where's the nearest drey?"

"I . . . we . . . we live in the Temple Tree. It's through there." He pointed to the track through the wood, now rapidly disappearing under a white blanket.

"Take me there, quickly, before we freeze," Tansy commanded him.

Chip looked at the tangle of hay-wire, felt the cold of the snow penetrating his fur and, with Tansy close behind, made for the Temple.

Crag, arranging metal in the hollow trunks, looked up as they entered in a flurry of snowflakes.

"Where's your offering?" he asked coldly.

Chip diverted his attention by introducing Tansy.

"Father, this is Tansywistful. I met her on the track. It is freezing cold and 'snow' outside."

"So, you abandoned your duty for a female and because you are a bit chilly. Huh!" Contempt sounded in every word. Crag turned away.

Soon, however, the Temple filled with cold grey squirrels who had returned with Rusty when conditions outside had made it impossible for them to "work their service". Tansy sat in a dark corner behind Chip, watching the Greys eating their meagre rations and rubbing their paws together to warm them. Crag and Rusty ignored her, but Chip fetched her two hazelnuts from the store area. Ivy watched.

As it got completely dark inside the tree, Tansy heard Crag call for silence for the Evening Prayer.

Invincible Sun,
Forgive us, your poor squirrels,
For always failing.

Tomorrow, we will,
If you will give us the strength,
Try to do better.

Tansy thought that his voice was colder than the snow outside.

"Do you snug up with the Greys?" she whispered to Chip.

The word was new to him and he savoured it; it had a warm, soft feel. "What is 'snug'?" he whispered back.

"You know, cuddle up in the dark."

"Cuddle up" sounded even nicer. He thought he knew what she meant. "No, we must all sleep apart," he told her.

"Nonsense," she told him, putting her paws around his shivering body and drawing him to her in the darkness. Then she settled down to cuddle him through the night, her tail fluffed and warm over them both.

They were still like that when Crag found them in the first thin light of a bitter winter's day.

"Out, out," he raged. "Sinners have no place in this Temple. The Sun will never, never forgive such behaviour. You, you squirrabel you, corrupting my son! Out, out! It's the Sunless Pit for you both. For ever!"

The confused female and the frightened young male were jostled and hustled out of the relative warmth of the tree into a cold white world outside.

"Follow me," Tansy said, hopping across the frozen crust of the snow which had hardened in the night. "We will go and find my friends."

"What are friends?" Chip asked.

Chapter 15

On the island Blood had scented the snow on the wind. In Scotland, where he had been captured the previous winter, he had often experienced snow and knew that the best thing to do then was to eat well and lie up.

The smell of peafowl drifted up from the nave below him, but he wanted *squirrel.* It had been a few days since he had outwitted the silly creatures when they had tried that same trick again. Did they think he was a stupid fox or something?

He came down the rope eagerly, snatched at the peacock's tailfeathers in passing, just to remind him that he was not to be ignored, and, as the frightened bird screeched in terror, slipped out through the door and up into the trees.

Once again there were no ruddled squirrels at the leaf-pile and he was pleased. Squirrel tasted much better when its blood was really warm from a good chase, and the hunt itself would be exhilarating.

He leapt from tree to tree, sniffing at the air, but even at Beech Valley there was no recent scent. He went along the Man-track up the centre of the island without even a glimpse of a squirrel's tail, and then, as the snow came drifting in on the north-east wind, he gave up the hunt and turned for home and peahen.

After Maple had been outwitted, and eaten in full view of the squirrels of Beech Valley, despair had overcome them. Oak the Cautious, feeling his age in the cold wind blowing in from the sea, had called a Council Meeting, sensing the need to provide stability and purpose in the shattered community.

In any crisis
A Leader's first duty is –
To keep hope alive.

They met in the pines well to the west of Beech Valley, which they now felt was unsafe and dangerous. Watchers were set out and the wary animals discussed ideas to counter the threat posed by the pine marten and enable them to survive.

"It could wipe uz all out," Just Poplar said. "Then there would be no zquirrelz to bury the nutz to make treez to feed future generationz of zquirrelz."

"There wouldn't be any future generations to feed," said Clover the Tagger and Carer in a despairing voice, and the bleakness of a squirrel-empty island overcame them all.

They sat silently, the chill wind tugging at their tails. Then Just Poplar, remembering his Royal days, said, "The Bunker!"

They turned to face him for an explanation.

"Uz don't know if it'z ztill there, but there uzed to be a hollow willow in the deepezd part of the Zwamp with one zmall entranze. It wuz known only to uz Royalz and won or two very truzded zervantz. It wuz where uz Royalz wuz all to go if the zervantz revolted. Uz wuz zhown it only wonz."

"Could you find it again?" asked Oak, eagerly.

"Uz could try, but uz wuz zhown it only wonz."

"Let's go now," said Oak, uncharacteristically, and the meeting broke up without even asking the Sun to bless its deliberations, the squirrels streaming off behind Just Poplar in the direction of the Zwamp.

They searched every mature willow, working their way through the trees above the black pools of water, until Poplar, with an urgent flicking of his tail, signalled success and the others, seeing this, joined him.

It was a perfect hiding place. The old tree leaned out across a pool and high up on its underside was a hole just big enough for a squirrel to enter. But, to get to it, the animals had to climb upside down along the trunk, clinging to the bark, with a drop into the pool below for any that lost a claw-hold.

Just Poplar went in first and flushed out a family of wrens who had regarded it as their winter home. They flew into the ivy covering a nearby alder stump, complaining amongst themselves in their thin voices.

Just Poplar hung his head out of the hole. "Come on in," he called. "Thiz *iz* the Bunker."

It was warm and dry inside, with plenty of room for the entire community. At the back of the hollow they found the old store-pile of nuts that the Royals had prepared for emergency use. Oak tried one; it was stale but edible.

They set a guard at the entrance and relaxed for the first time in a moon. They were even more glad of the protection of the Bunker when the east wind swirled the snowflakes past the entrance hole.

Chapter 16

Chip followed "Tansywistful" across the snowdrifts in the Lightning Tree clearing. The night wind had whipped the snow into fantastic shapes and had hardened and compacted the surface, before dropping to a whisper and fading away with the dawn.

The two squirrels travelled mostly through the treetops but, when they had to come down, they hopped around the great banks and curls of snow which sparkled and twinkled as the light from the rising sun coloured the drifts first pink, then gold.

Tansy showed Chip the marks left by the night animals; the fine footprints of a fox and the yellow spots where it had marked its passage across its territory. She showed him the splayed wing-marks where a heavy bird had taken to the air at the end of a line of backward-pointing arrows, and the golden feather with the dark band that identified it as a pheasant. All across the snow were the marks of two long and two round footprints.

"What made those?" Chip asked her.

"Rabbits," she told him.

"What are rabbits?"

Tansy looked at him in surprise. "Brown-furred creatures with long ears that live in holes in the ground."

"So *that's* what they are called. My father would never say their name. On Portland he said it was a Sun-cursed word and must never be spoken."

"What did he call them, then?" Tansy asked.

"Brown-furred creatures with long ears that live in holes in the ground," he replied, and they both laughed, their breath white in the air.

"Rabbits, rabbits, rabbits. What a funny word," he said.

The two went on together, each comforted by the other's presence, the snow-crust supporting them easily. Chip poked at his ears as they seemed not to be hearing properly; Tansy pointed out that this was the "snow-silence" and all sounds would seem muffled. They came to the top of a bank and looked down on to the pool, not blue that morning but covered in windswept grey ice, and they skirted it, keeping to the treetops.

"I'm expecting Marguerite to have a drey somewhere about here,' Tansy told Chip, and they searched each likely tree. She was right. A snug drey, nestled in a dense mass of pine branches and twigs, showed signs of habitation. Tansy called from outside,

> *"Hello and greetings.*
> *We visit you and bring peace.*
> *Emerge or we leave."*

She used the ancient Calling Kernel which enabled any squirrel inside to greet or to ignore visitors to the drey, according to that resident's mood.

"Who calls?" a sleepy voice responded.

"Tansy the Wistful," she replied, a slight catch in her voice, "from Ourland, and Chip Who Has No Tag."

"Tansy!" An excited voice came from within the drey and Marguerite pushed herself out and instantly brushed whiskers with her old friend and year-mate.

"Tansy!"

"Marguerite!" They were hugging and whisker-brushing in a display of emotion never before witnessed by the shivering young male beside them.

"I'm sorry," Marguerite said at last, remembering her manners, and she made the formal greeting to him, adding, "Come in out of the cold." Then she said to Tansy, "Meet my youngsters and Juniper. You'll remember him, of course. Come on in, both of you."

Chip followed them into the cosy warmth of the drey and met Juniper the Steadfast, Marguerite's life-mate, and Oak and Burdock, their youngsters. It was crowded inside, each squirrel closely in contact with the others, but with no sense of sinning in the contact. In fact, Chip was overwhelmed by the cared-for feeling; the whole drey was filled with it.

He thawed out in the semi-darkness as he listened to Tansy tell of the reason for her journey.

"Marguerite, have you still got the Woodstock?" she asked as soon as it was decently possible.

"Not the original one, but yes, there is still a Woodstock. We keep it hidden. Why do you ask?"

"There's a pine marten on Ourland killing all the squirrels. I have come to get the Woodstock to kill it."

"How did you cross the sea from Ourland?" Marguerite asked, remembering her journey in the rubber boat and the help the dolphins gave when she and her companions were in trouble amongst the rock towers.

Tansy told Marguerite of the stag, and of being caught and held in the cage. "But I'm here now, thank the Sun. All I've got to do is get the Woodstock back to Ourland and kill the pine marten."

"That's a big, 'all'," said Marguerite, thinking as she said it that she sounded like her father, Oak the Cautious. "Have you thought how you would get it there?"

"No, not really. I had to get *here* first," Tansy replied bleakly, and added, "but I'll find a way."

Marguerite pressed Tansy for details of her own family on the island. Chip could tell that she was astonished to hear of the death of Next-King Sallow and the abdication of King Willow and his other son, Just Poplar.

Then it was Marguerite's turn to tell of her adventures after leaving the island, of the friendly dolphins, and of meeting the refugees at Worbarrow. Then of the destruction of the Greys' Power Square in the Clay-Pan. This brought them to the "Grey" situation, and Tansy asked what Marguerite knew about them now.

"A plague that they called the Grey Death killed all of the ones that were here at that time, except Marble, and he died nobly trying to help us destroy the Power Square. Then, in late autumn, more came, very polite and friendly, but we sent them to the North-east Wood for the winter. They said that they wanted to live with us and learn our customs, but we didn't trust them, and winter was nearly here. If they come back in the spring, we will talk with them then. You didn't meet them when you came through there?"

Tansy told of meeting Chip near the Lightning Tree and of the Greys, and finally about being ejected by Chip's father, Crag, for snugging with Chip. The Reds were aghast at this, so Chip tried to explain the Portlanders' customs. He was hesitant in the company of so many others, and their proximity troubled him a little. Their body contact and ease of speech seemed to him to be wrong in some ways, but right, oh, so beautifully right, in others. Finally he asked the question that was troubling him.

"What is this feeling here? Every squirrel seems to care for every other squirrel."

Marguerite looked at the youngster, pathetic in his concern. She leaned over, brushed whiskers with him and whispered, "We call it Loving."

Chapter 17

Crag was fretting. The sun was shining and he knew that he should be out with his team of Greys getting more and more metal for the Temple. Yet the whole of his world was covered in this Sun-damned snow.

He sent for Hickory and Sitka and instructed them to organise the Greys in rearranging the offerings in the hollows of the tree. Then, dissatisfied, he had them put all the pieces back where they had been before. The Greys grumbled amongst themselves and he had to threaten the Sunless Pit to keep them active and Sun-worthy. Rusty was as silent as usual, but Crag could sense her resentment at the way he had treated Chip and that female who had spent the night with the youngster in the Temple Tree.

What else could he, Crag the Temple Master, have done? Chip might be his son, but building up the offerings in the Temple must always be his main concern, and the Greys seemed easily led and open to any influence. He dared not let standards drop, even for a moment. He was sure that the youngster would be back, suitably contrite and begging to be forgiven, when he found how degenerate other squirrels were. He was sure that he had taught him well.

Training is vital.
As the growing twig is bent –
So shall the tree grow.

Crag moved a rusted gate-latch to a new position, studied it for a minute, then moved it back a nut-width.

Ivy watched Crag moving the metal about. There was something in the intensity of his movements that impressed her. He really did believe in what he was doing. When she found an opportunity, she would ask him what it all meant.

Across the bright snow-covered heath and the cold marshes, beyond the leaden waters of Poole Harbour, in the chill belltower of the disused church, Blood woke and stretched himself, prowled about in the tiny room that was now home to him and decided he would go outside, if only to look around.

He came down the rope into the smelly nave, brightly lit in an unusual way by the reflected sunlight from the snow outside, and assessed his living larder. There were enough of the silly birds to see him through to the spring, even if he couldn't find squirrel again.

The biggest cock bird, known to his harem as Mogul, whose tail swept to the floor, eyed him sleepily.

I'll keep you till last, Blood thought. You're probably tough and stringy anyway. In passing, he pulled out a tail feather with his teeth and, ignoring the squawk of protest, carried it outside, where the sun caught the feather's rainbow eye and even Blood had to admire the iridescent colours.

Moved by an unusual urge, he poked the feather upright

into a snowdrift and pranced around it, making a ring of tracks in the crisp surface, then set off towards the leaf-pile in the swamp, mocked on his way by a pair of magpies, their white undersides appearing dingy against the gleaming brilliance of the snow.

After his first two visits he had never found squirrels at the leaf-pile, but it was worth a try, and he always went that way on his squirrel-hunting expeditions.

The ex-zervant, Caterpillar, in the Bunker, was bored. He had heard all the stories of Acorn, the first squirrel in the world, that any of them there knew. He had listened to endless discussions on new games for the ex-zervantz to replace the creepy-crawly names given to them by the Royals and thought the whole business unnecessary. He had refused the proposal of Catalpa for himself. He had always been Caterpillar and had never even seen a catalpa tree. He doubted very much if such a tree really existed!

And as for a tag – not for him! He would probably end up as Caterpillar the Ruddled, as all the Ourlanders knew of his fondness for the fermented sloes.

A diffused light was filling the hollow of the tree. The pool below was covered in ice and snow and the sunlight was reflected by this up through the round entrance. Caterpillar went and looked out of the hole, the light in the Bunker dimming as his head nearly filled the opening. "I'm going out", he called back over his shoulder.

In the early Bunker days the squirrels, when they needed to drink or to dispose of their meagre droppings, had always gone out in pairs, one to be watchful all the time.

A watchful squirrel
Survives to breed and father –
More watchful squirrels.

Despite the strength of this Kernel, in the absence of any attack or even a sighting of the marten since they had been in the Bunker, some of the squirrels had relaxed and gone out singly, but never for more than a few leaps from the leaning willow trunk. Today most of them were in the semi-dormant state that is not true hibernation, but does reduce the body's calls on the fat-reserves. Oak saw Caterpillar go, but was not concerned; he would be back soon.

Blood bounded along, the midwinter sun just warm on his back, his eyes narrowed against the glare from the snow. The air felt crisp and clean in his nostrils. There was no scent of squirrel as he came to the leaf-pile, dark in the white expanse, where the heat of the decaying leaves had melted the night's covering. He playfully scattered the compost, kicking it backwards from the pile and seeing how far he could spread it; the rotting leaves made brown stains on the white blanket.

As he dug down he found small round fruit, warm from the leaf-heat and smelling like the squirrels he had first found here. He tasted one whilst the magpies chattered and scolded him from a nearby bush. The fruit warmed his tongue, like blood, but as he swallowed, the warmth continued down his throat and exploded inside him. Wow!

He took another bite, and then another. He ate three of the sloes before the trees leaned over sideways and the magpies grew to the size of the eagles he could remember from Scotland. Blood did not care a feather. He ate another of the ruddled fruit.

Caterpillar, his sloe-craving overriding discipline or fear, climbed out from the Bunker entrance and along the underside of the trunk, then dropped to the snow-covered ground. No other squirrel had followed him out. In the muffled silence he stood on a drift and sniffed the air. Nothing, just snow and trees. He looked up at the hole, took a mouthful of snow, cold and crisp, felt it melt on his tongue, then hopped off in the direction of the leaf-pile.

He heard the magpies' warning long before he reached it. It was their "four-footed predator" call, so he climbed an alder trunk and went slowly through the bare branches, from tree to tree, until he could see them fluttering about in a bush near the leaf-pile, on which lay a ruddled pine marten.

Even with his traditional foe so far below him and obviously harmless, he felt the paralysing marten-dread seize him and he had to shake it off consciously. Caterpillar sat there, for the first time able to study their enemy with safety.

The pine marten lay on its back, apparently oblivious to the magpies who were growing bolder and circling closer, their harsh chatter annoying Caterpillar, who now dared to come a long way down the trunk. The magpies saw his movement and, suddenly tiring of their game with no response from the hunter, flew off together through the trees. Caterpillar waited and watched in the silence.

Slowly it dawned on him that the scourge of Ourland, the

terror which had haunted them for so long and which had forced them to live in that Sun-damned Bunker, was lying ruddled and helpless on the leaf-pile below him.

Had he been born a free squirrel, he might have known what to do, but being an ex-zervant, he had been trained from birth not to think for himself, just to do as he was instructed and to report unusual happenings to the Royals.

This was an unusual happening, but there were no Royals now, and if he told Oak the Cautious, their Council Leader, he might insist on punishing him with a denigratory tag for going so far from the Bunker against orders.

So Caterpillar sat there indecisively, and watched the pine marten as the sun's shadow moved round; until, chilled by a cold breeze from the sea, he turned back for the Bunker. Oak was waiting, concerned at his long absence.

"What kept you?" he asked, his voice as cold as the air outside. "Have you been to the leaf-pile?"

Oak manoeuvred himself until he could smell the errant squirrel's breath, but there was no taint of the ruddled sloes.

Caterpillar toyed with a full lie – zervantz were adept at these – then, seeing a slight relaxation in Oak's stance, chose the half-lie.

"Uz wuz bored and ztiff and uz went for a little exerzize," he said.

"To the leaf-pile?" Oak asked, knowing the habits of the ex-zervantz.

"Well, uz did go that way," Caterpillar conceded, then decided to turn the inquisition away from herself and said, "The marten wuz there, him udd been at the zloez."

"Martens don't eat fruit," Oak challenged him.

"Thiz won doez. Thoroughly ruddled, him wuz, lying of hiz back there like a dreyling, gone to thiz world."

"When was this?" snapped Oak.

Caterpillar looked around, trying to judge time from the artificially small amount of light coming in through the entrance hole. "A while pazd," was all he could say.

The other squirrels were alert now and had gathered round, aware of a feeling of excitement. Oak declared a Council Meeting.

"Caterpillar has reported that our enemy is senseless at the leaf-pile. This is an opportunity we must examine. What suggestions are there?"

"Let'z all go and kill it," said Just Poplar at once.

"Hold on," said Oak, his cautious nature asserting itself. "It may be a trap.

Squirrels – to survive
Never act impulsively.
Look before you leap."

To which Just Poplar replied, quoting a Kernel that Old Burdock had taught him,

"Fear can paralyze.
Zupprezz it and ACT. He who
Hezitatez iz lozd."

They looked to the Tagger, Clover, for clarification.

"Those Kernels do seem to contradict one another," she said. "I wish Old Burdock were here; she knew how to resolve these things. I suppose that it depends on the exact circumstances. Now if . . ."

The arguments went back and forth, the light in the Bunker dimming all the time.

Finally, Oak remembered the Leaders' Kernel:

Indecision kills.
Act positively and lead.
Action is the Key.

"We'll go and kill the Marten," he said, then, realising that in a few minutes it would be completely dark outside, added, "in the morning."

Blood awoke. It was warm on the leaf-pile but the magpies were now *inside* his head and chattering incessantly. He stood up, fell over, then stood up more slowly. It was dark. He moved on to the snow and pushed his face into the coolness of a drift. The magpies in his head were not quite so loud now and, as he headed unsteadily for home, they almost, but not quite, stopped pecking at the inside of his skull.

At the door of the church he paused, pushed his face into the snow once more, pulled the peacock feather from the snowdrift and urinated on it, then went into the dark nave. He brushed against Mogul's tail, thought of giving it the usual tug, but his head told him that it could not take the inevitable screech.

He tried to climb the rope to his den in the tower. After the third fall he gave up, crawled under a pew and slept noisily amongst the dry peacock droppings and feather moult.

Chapter 18

Tansy had pressed Marguerite to tell her when the Woodstock could be taken to Ourland to deal with the pine marten on the assumption that, with her own parents in danger, Marguerite would drop everything and leave at once.

Marguerite's first reaction had been to do just that, and her busy mind started to organise the venture. Then she realised that she was not a free agent. She was the selected Tagger of this community, responsible for important aspects of their lives. She also had youngsters of her own, rather young for the hazards of winter travelling. It would need more than the efforts of Tansy and herself to take the Woodstock any distance. This, and the unknown future behaviour of Chip's family and the Greys, made the whole project impossible. But then she had been taught that nothing is impossible. The Kernel said:

If you think you can
Or if you think you cannot,
Either way it's true.

So far she had not thought that she could.

"Tansy-Friend," she said, "we *will* find a way to get rid of the pine marten, but there is a lot of planning to be done first. There are many details for me to work out. Rest and sleep while I think about these. Nothing more can be done while this snow lasts. Try to sleep now. Leave it to me."

Juniper had been watching the shadows of the trees at High Sun as they reached out across the snow-covered ice on the Blue Pool. "They're getting shorter," he reported. "The Longest Night is gone. We can have the Midwinter Celebrations any time now."

Chip was exquisitely warm in the drey, constantly and pleasurably aware of the close contact with the other squirrels, especially Tansywistful, who was in a deep sleep next to him. He asked in a whisper, "What happens to the Sun in midwinter?"

Marguerite explained. "Every autumn the Sun, who is tired after shining so hard for us all summer, finds it harder and harder to climb up high in the sky. But, in the middle of the winter, his strength starts to come back, ready for the next year.

"We can tell when this is, because the shadows at High Sun start to get shorter. We celebrate then, because we know that spring and summer are on the way, and that winter will not last for ever." She smiled at the inquisitive youngster, encouraging him to ask another question.

"What's a celebration?"

"That's when all the squirrels get together to thank the Sun and enjoy themselves. We have feasting on our favourite foods, play games and chases and tell stories, usually about Acorn, the first squirrel in the world."

"And Primrose – who wouldn't go in the boat?" Chip asked.

"Yes. Do you know that story?" Marguerite sounded surprised.

Chip remembered that he had heard it when listening secretly with his parents that September night and, guided by an instinctive loyalty, replied, "Yes, I have heard it somewhere", and followed immediately with, "Where do you have these celebration things?"

"It has to be outside, for all of us to get together. That's why the winter one is sometimes late. We have to wait for a warm enough day."

The snow lay for three days, then a warm south-westerly wind came, with rain on its back, and the drifts shrank to dirty ridges before disappearing altogether. In the mild spell that followed the Celebrations were held.

Tansy tried to join in, but her mind was away on Ourland. The funny little squirrel she had brought away from the Cold Ones in the hollow tree stayed near her most of the time, always asking questions. A male of her own year, Tamarisk the Forthright, was also paying her attention and making disparaging remarks about Chip whenever he saw an opportunity.

"Why do you spend so much time with that little sqrunt?" he had asked her whilst Chip was within ear-twitch.

"He *needs* me more than you do – Mouth!" she replied.

"That's a matter of opinion," replied Tamarisk, immediately regretting his remark as Tansy turned her back on him, her tail indicating only too clearly that she had nothing more to say. He sulked away. Tansy's thoughts turned back to the pine marten and what she might have to do to get Marguerite to take some action.

Crag had waited for Chip to return to the Temple Tree, assuring Rusty that it must be the snow that was keeping him from his duties, and that his training and his fear of the Sunless Pit would bring him back. When the snow was gone and the weather had improved, however, Crag left the Greys and Rusty collecting metal, and went alone to the Blue Pool.

The colour startled him as the pool came in sight, azure under the clear winter sky, and he almost allowed himself a moment of pleasurable appreciation, but this was soon mastered and he pressed on with the task in hand: finding his errant son and bringing him back to help collect the sacred metal.

The Greys were now proving to be troublesome and lazy, not working as hard as he wished, and idling if he was not there to supervise. The metal store in the Temple was not growing as fast as he wanted it to. *Every* paw was needed.

One female, Ivy, obviously older than the others, had been asking questions. Why did they collect the metal? How long had they been doing it? Why did they come to this part of the country near other red squirrels but not have anything to do with them? Did red females ever hold equal positions to males?

It was this last question that Crag had found hardest to answer. There had never been females on Portland who had been anything other than producers of young squirrels, and more recently metal collectors, and they had not been good at either of these duties. Even Rusty had only ever managed to produce one dreyling, and he was a disappointment. Rusty was not much use at collecting metal either.

This female at the Blue Pool, though, who called herself Marguerite, appeared to hold a position and have equality. It must be a part of their degenerate ways. He had told Ivy that females were not capable of holding responsible positions, but they could be Sun-worthy and avoid the Sunless Pit if they worked hard at collecting the sacred metal.

Crag didn't meet any squirrels as he passed through the Deepend Guardianship, but on nearing Steepbank he stopped and watched. There were squirrels, red ones like himself, playing and sporting in the branches. That strange feeling, for which he had no name, was spreading out and trying to affect even him. He tensed his muscles to resist it. Were these degenerate ones always misbehaving?

Looking for Chip, he saw him following that squirrabel who had decoyed him from his home and duties, and a disturbing thought struck him. Could they have mated?

They were of different years, but that was no physical barrier. It would be awful if they had. However much one tried not to enjoy THAT, it did create a bond and it would be that much harder to get his son back. Sun forbid that he had mated with a Blasphemer.

Crag thought of the Portland "Bill", decreed by his grandfather, which clearly stated that the mating act was to take place only once each year and was not to be enjoyed. His great-grandfather had also, in that Bill, decreed that there was to be no frivolity, none of the traditional chasing and courting. The act must be done coldly and soberly, as befits true believers and collectors.

He, Crag, had kept to the Bill, but had to admit that it was hard not to enjoy mating, even with a dry old stick like Rusty. Evidently other Portland squirrels hadn't acted correctly and that was why the Sun had punished them with no offspring.

He approached the playful party and was seen by Chip, who moved closer to Tansy, who had reluctantly joined in when she could see that Marguerite would need time to organise a rescue party. Even so, to her the joviality seemed wrong and out of place.

Alder the Leader went along the branch to greet the squirrel stranger who had come to join them on this happy day.

"Greetings, stranger. I am Alder the Leader, selected Senior Squirrel in this our Demesne of the Blue Pool. I welcome you to our Midwinter Celebrations." He waited for the formal reply.

Crag scowled at the squirrels all about him.

"I am Crag, father of that idler," he said, pointing to Chip, who was cowering on a branch beside Tansy, "and I have come to take him back with me."

Alder stared at Crag and was silent in the face of this discourtesy. He had made allowances when the foreign Greys did not know of the correct greetings and customs, but this was a Red like himself, who ought to know the routines!

All the other squirrels looked on in silence until Marguerite said, "Stranger, your attitude puzzles and offends us. We have offered you our hospitality, yet you ignore this and insult your own youngster. If Chip wishes to leave with you, that is his right, now he is of age, but I for one would not blame him if he didn't." She flicked her tail to show contempt for his lack of manners and quoted the Kernel:

After Longest Night
Last year's youngsters can decide
Their own destinies.

Crag ignored her, "Come," he ordered, glowering at Chip, who was still crouching at Tansy's side. She put a paw on his shoulder. He started to obey his father, but, feeling the pressure from Tansy's paw increase, replied, "I choose to stay."

Crag moved forward, then stopped and turned to go. He called back, "It's the Sunless Pit for you, *and* the rest of you. For ever!" His grand exit was spoilt by his missing a paw-hold in his anger and having to drop to a lower branch.

Moving from tree to tree in as dignified a way as he could, back towards the North-east Wood and the Temple Tree, he felt a resurgence of the squirrelation overtake him and, out of sight of the others, he paused irresolutely. There can be no harm in watching what they are up to, he told himself, an old saying of his grandfather's rising to his mind:

Know your enemy.
Find out all his weaknesses.
These will be your strengths.

He circled round to hide downwind of the revellers and observe, but if he had hoped for a true view he was disappointed. The dampening effect of his visit had spoilt the day for most of them, and soon, in an attempt to divert the squirrels' attention, Alder called on his life-mate, Dandelion, to tell an Acorn story. The squirrels gathered around her in the late-afternoon sunshine. Crag moved up quietly to listen, unobserved.

Dandelion looked around, saw that they were all seated and ready and began.

"Once upon a time, on the great rock of Portland, lived Acorn and Primrose. This was a long time after the Flood had come and gone, and hardly any animals lived there because there was not much soil on the rock to grow plants to feed them. The sequoia tree in which they lived was beginning to die as its roots were not able to find enough soil and moisture to feed it.

" 'Let's go and find another place to live,' " Acorn suggested, and his eyes lit up with excitement at the thought, as he always enjoyed an adventure. Primrose was not so ready to leave her home, though she was eager to see more of the new world. Acorn had to explain about the dying tree and how he was sure that there would be many lovely places on the Mainland, which he described as growing with nuts, and sunny, though in fact he had never been there. Even squirrels like Acorn will sometimes describe things in autumn colours when they want to persuade others to do something.

"Now, when my grandfather told me this story I had no real idea of how a squirrel would get from Portland to the Mainland, but Young Chip, who used to live there, has told me all about it. Portland is called an island, but it is not really an island because there is a bank of pebbles, round like birds' eggs, joining it to the Mainland. Acorn and Primrose set off along these pebbles, with Acorn telling Primrose not to look back – there was adventure and excitement ahead.

"As he was telling her this, a great wave came rushing up the beach and swept Acorn out to sea."

"I saw waves like that," said Chip. "They are huge!"

The other squirrels turned to him and Tansy whispered, "You are not supposed to interrupt when a story is being told, Chip-Friend."

"I'm sorry," he said, "but it is just like that. Sorry."

Dandelion smiled at the apologetic youngster. Obviously his family did not tell such stories to one another.

"Where was I? Oh, yes. Acorn had been swept out to sea by the wave and Primrose was left on the beach, heart-broken because she was sure that her beloved Acorn would drown, and she could not swim out to rescue him. However, the Sun knew that if he let Acorn drown, then there could be no more squirrels, as they were still the only ones in the world. So he sent a *second* wave to sweep Primrose out as well. She was terrified, but this wave took her right to Acorn's side where she clung on to him so that he couldn't swim either, and they both started to sink.

"Suddenly, up from underneath them came a big black shape that lifted them out of the water. From near their feet a hole opened and a fountain of water shot up into the sky. Then air hissed down into the hole it had come out of. It was a . . ."

"A whale!" shouted Chip and, as every squirrel turned towards him again, he said, "Sorry, but I saw one once.

They are black and they live in the sea and they are ever so big . . . Sorry."

"I didn't know if they really existed outside stories," admitted Dandelion, "but if Chip has seen one, then they must. Thank you, Chip.

"Now, this whale was very big and whether or not it knew it had two squirrels on its back, Acorn and Primrose couldn't tell. They were afraid that it would sink again and they would be back drowning in the sea. However, this whale started to swim around Portland just as if it did know that it was carrying something very important and knew just where it had to go.

"Acorn and Primrose clung to each other, trying to keep their balance on the smooth skin of the whale as there was nothing else to hold on to. They were afraid that if they dug their claws in, the whale would dive under the water to get them to stop.

"When the whale had swum past the end of Portland, it turned and swam towards some white cliffs, then along the coast for a very long way until it passed a long sandy beach on their left-paw side and through a narrow place where the sea was rushing out. Ahead was an island which Acorn thought was the most beautiful island he had ever seen, with trees reaching out over the water. Under one of these trees the whale stopped, and Acorn and Primrose climbed up an overhanging branch and on to the island. The whale flipped its tail at them, then swam back out to sea.

" 'What is this place called?' " Primrose asked, as she believed that Acorn knew everything.

"He looked around with a knowing look on his face. 'This is Our Land,' " he said.

"And that is how squirrels first came to Ourland and they are still there, as several of you know. Wood Anemone and Spindle were born there." Dandelion looked for the ex-zerventz amongst her audience.

"That'z true," said Spindle, "but it zeemz a long while now zinze."

The listening squirrels flicked their tails as a sign of appreciation to the story-teller and, with some of the young ones yawning and stretching, they went off to their dreys as the sun dipped below the horizon and a chill spread through the winter air.

Crag sat on his hidden branch feeling the cold penetrate his fur. What subversive rot! What rubbish! How could any squirrel believe that? Squirrels being carried on the backs of whales, indeed. Rubbish!

Hunger pangs stabbed at his gut and he dropped to the ground to forage in the dusk. This was one of the places those two naïve squirrels had told him was a store area. He could scent plentiful supplies of buried nuts, hidden by the Blasphemers in the autumn. If my work-team had this food, he thought, they would not have to waste precious metal-carrying time foraging. These Blasphemers and tellers of false stories didn't deserve the Sun's bounty.

He turned and made his way to the Temple. He would have to work extra hard tomorrow to make up for a wasted day, but the Grey team would work better with full stomachs.

Chapter 19

The squirrels in the Bunker had nearly finished the food reserves. Oak had rationed the stale nuts from the first day they had been in the hollow tree and, as all of them were well fed and winter-fat from a plentiful autumn, there had been no real hardship, though Fern the Fussy had constantly complained about the rancid taste of some of the shrivelled old kernels. Oak had had to take her to one side and point out that as the life-mate of the Leader she was expected to set an example to the others.

At first morale had been good; the relief at being in a place away from the constant fear of attack by the pine marten was enough. But when Caterpillar had failed to tell them in time that the marten was vulnerable, and each of the senior squirrels knew that they all shared responsibility for the indecision, many found it easier to blame the individual who had been first at fault. Caterpillar felt himself to be isolated and stayed on his own in a far corner of the hollow.

The ex-Royals – Just Poplar, his mother, Ex-Kingz-Mate Thizle, and his sister, Teazle, as well as his cousins, Voxglove, Cowzlip and Fir – tended to keep together in a group, though Voxglove and Cowzlip were learning all they could from Clover about the craft of being a Carer. Fir would occasionally mix with the incomers, but he did not have much to do with the ex-zervantz.

Amongst the others, liaisons formed and dissolved in the confines of the hollow tree, most ending in harsh words and sulks; the confined space of the Bunker distorted the courting patterns evolved over centuries of open space and tree-life.

Oak guessed that the Longest Night must have passed, and suggested to Fern that they hold some kind of celebration.

Fern was having another bad day; she hated the darkness of the hollow. "With what?" she had replied, witheringly. "Stale hazelnuts and a mouthful of fungus each? Forget it!"

As the days passed, the quarrels increased and Oak knew that some action on his part was needed, but he was unsure what to do and was therefore pleased when another cold spell made all the confined squirrels sink into a semi-dormant state, bringing peace to the Bunker once more.

One morning, as the light in the hollow was beginning to brighten with the rising sun, Just Poplar gently shook Oak's shoulder to waken him.

"I think your Fern is Sun-gone," he said.

Oak turned and looked at his life-mate curled beside him and shook her gently. She didn't stir. Her tail, with the thin grey hairs of age, covered her as a blanket. He hadn't noticed how old she had been looking until then and he felt a twinge of vulnerability as he realised that he too was really quite old now. He shook her again, not believing that she could just have left him in the night, then called Clover to see to her. She confirmed that Fern the Fussy was indeed Sun-gone.

Memories of happier days at the Blue Pool flooded over him. He could picture her sitting on the grooming branch outside their drey there, combing her fur and tail with her claws. Everything had to be just so!

All he could do now was to ensure that she had a worthy burial. Somewhere peaceful where she could nourish a tree, as it said in the Farewell Kernel:

Sun, take this squirrel
Into the peace of your earth
To nourish a tree.

Clover was clearly thinking the same thing. She opened her mouth as though to say the Kernel, closed it again, looked across at the entrance hole and then said, "We've got a problem."

Oak was about to respond by quoting the Kernel which stated that there were no Problems, only Challenges, thought better of it and waited for Clover to explain.

"We *can't* bury Fern," she said. "As soon as we get her through the hole, she'll drop into the swamp."

"We can't keep her in here," Oak replied, and looked at Just Poplar as if he might know how the body could be disposed of in a dignified and fitting way.

The other squirrels had woken and were gathered round Oak with words of comfort and regret. An informal Council Meeting developed and finally it was agreed, with Oak grudgingly conceding, that they would, for the sake of the enclosed community, *have* to drop the body out of the hole into the zwamp.

Fern would not have liked that, Oak thought, remembering how carefully she had groomed herself each day, determined to maintain what she called "proper standards", but he could see no alternative.

Fern's body was dragged to the exit hole and Clover rehearsed the Farewell Kernel in her mind. It was not exactly appropriate, she thought – squirrels like to be buried at the foot of their favourite tree – but times were not normal. She looked at the other squirrels clustered around her in the dim light, then reached out and put her paw on Fern's shoulder. Clover opened her mouth and was about to say the Kernel when Chestnut the Doubter, who had kept silent up to this point, whispered in her ear, "I don't think she'll go through the hole."

Chestnut was right. The body had stiffened in the curled-up sleeping position, and would not straighten. No manoeuvring or shoving could post it to a muddy and undignified end. As the squirrels always buried their Sun-gone ones at once, they were not to know that if they had waited, their problem would have solved itself. Even in death Fern had managed to maintain "proper standards".

A formal Council Meeting was convened and after an awkward discussion it was decided that, as tradition called for bodies to be buried as soon as possible after death, they had no choice other than to dig a hole in the powdery punkwood at the very furthest corner of the hollow and put Fern in that. Oak and Clover said the Farewell Kernel together as the other squirrels crouched silently around them. Then Oak, suddenly needing to be alone, went out through the exit hole and climbed up the bark of the old willow to the highest branch, where he clung blinking in the bright sunlight.

Chapter 20

Crag sensed a different atmosphere in the Temple Tree when he awoke. There was an ominous grumbling from the Greys and he knew that whilst he had been away they had been plotting against him. Why had Rusty not warned him? Then he recalled that she *had* tried to talk to him the previous night. He had forbidden her to speak as he had been tired, and he had sent her off to her own sleeping space.

Hickory and Sitka were climbing up towards him, followed at a distance by that female, Ivy, or Poison Ivy as he had heard some of the Greys call her. They looked ill at ease.

Crag did not wait for them to speak. "I'm glad that you came up. I have an announcement to make. I am able to increase rations all round and today there will be no work. This is to be a Sin-day to celebrate the passing of the Longest Night."

Hickory glanced at Sitka, then turned back to Crag.

"What's a Sin-day?"

"It's a day when there is no work and we all have extra rations. Go and tell the others. There will be a special meal at dusk. In the meantime you may all rest or forage as you feel inclined. That is all." He dismissed the Greys with a flick of his tail and went outside. He hoped that the local sycamore trees were subject to the same afflictions as the few Portland ones had been.

They were. He sorted through the dead leaves on the ground until he had at least one for every Grey plus one each for himself and Rusty and carried these back to the Temple Tree, watched by Greys sitting about in unaccustomed idleness.

At dusk he called the Greys together and handed each a leaf. Then he gave one to Rusty and held one in his own paw.

"Do exactly as I do," he instructed as he rolled the leaf into a tight tube. He smiled as he did this and the Greys, intrigued by this previously unseen aspect of the Temple Master's character, relaxed, and tried to roll their crisp black-spotted leaf into a similar tight tube. Crag went from squirrel to squirrel, holding his own rolled leaf and directing the others as their tubes sprang open and they rolled them up again. For the first time, laughter was heard in the Temple Tree clearing.

Crag was showing Ivy just how it was done when his own leaf dropped from under his left forelimb and unrolled on the ground. He grabbed it quickly and rolled it tightly, but not before Ivy had seen that this leaf was clear of any of the black mould spots.

Crag moved among the Greys until every squirrel was holding a tightly rolled leaf.

"Now," he said loudly, "we must each eat our own leaf. Stem and all. Like this . . ." He nibbled his way rapidly down the leaf then chewed the brown stem. "There," he said, "nothing to it!"

The Greys, having some unaccustomed fun, followed him and, vying with each other to be the first, crunched on the musty-tasting leaves. Only Ivy, pretending to be having difficulty with her broken tooth, let her leaf unroll and bit at it carefully, unobtrusively dropping the pieces with the black spots on them.

In the night Hickory crawled across to Sitka's sleeping place.

"I feel awful," he whispered. "I know it can't be true, but I feel as if I'm falling through space, spinning round and round like a sycamore seed."

"Me too," said Sitka, and they crouched together, shivering and waiting for daylight.

For them and nearly all the other squirrels in the Temple Tree, daylight did not come that day. Long after they knew it must be light, the helpless, sick animals cowered in apparent darkness, blinking their blind eyes and clinging to the inside of the tree in a vain attempt to stop the spinning, falling feeling.

Ivy, the only unaffected Grey, watched Crag moving silently among them. She noted that Rusty was in the same state as the Greys.

At High-Sun Crag moved into a position where he could be heard by all.

"I am disappointed," he announced. "Not one of you has passed the Sin-test. Each of you must have sinned grievously to be so affected. This is why the test is special. It finds out not only the squirrel who has sinned openly, but those who have sinned in their hearts. All those who are impure will now be experiencing the horror of the Sunless Pit. Falling in darkness for ever. He paused. "But I, Crag the Temple Master, can give you hope. All those who truly repent and vow to serve the Sun in any way I direct will be forgiven and have a second chance. Think on what I have said."

He climbed out of the hollow and up one of the dying upper limbs of the oak. Ivy followed him.

"You misserable crooked worm and tricksster," she said, the words hissing savagely past her broken tooth. "I know that you made them eat poissoned leavess and that iss why they are all sick. Even your own mate. I don't know whether to kill you mysself or tell the otherss what you have done and let them do it."

She looked at Crag in contempt, then spoke again. "There iss, of coursse, one other thing you could do."

Crag looked up at her. She suddenly seemed much bigger than he was.

"You could tell the otherss that I alone have not sinned and becausse of thiss I am to be in charge of all the Greyss."

Crag hesitated.

"Right," said Ivy. "I will denounsse you for the tricksster you are."

"Wait," said Crag. "Tell me just what you want. I am sure that we can work together for the glory of the Sun."

"Ressponssibility," said Ivy, "and a chansse to prove mysself to otherss."

On the third morning after the Celebrations Juniper wriggled out of his drey in a pine overlooking the Blue Pool and started down the trunk to forage for his breakfast. He stopped, head down. The ground below him was covered with grey squirrels, scratching and digging where he and Marguerite had buried their winter reserves. He went carefully on down the tree to investigate, pausing a few feet above the scattered pine needles covering the earth.

"What are you doing?" he asked, the formal greeting seeming inappropriate.

The Greys ignored him. He asked again, and was again ignored as the intruders dug up nut after nut, eating some and preparing others to be carried away.

"What *are* you *doing*?" he asked loudly, for the third time.

None of the busy Greys so much as glanced in his direction. He looked round for support, but no other Red was in sight and he felt the same frustration that he had known when, as a dreyling, his companions had "sent him to the conker tree" for some misdemeanour or other. Juniper went back up the pine trunk to alert Marguerite.

Other Reds were now coming silently through the trees, warily watching the activity below. Soon Alder the leader arrived, leaping across the last gap and landing awkwardly, having no tail to balance himself with. The others looked to him for guidance.

"What's going on?" he asked.

Juniper explained what little he knew.

With Juniper and Marguerite beside him, Alder went down the trunk and asked the Greys why they were digging up all his community's nuts. Alder too was ignored; the Greys just carried on as if the Reds did not exist. Not knowing how to stop them, Alder, after a minute or so, led Juniper and Marguerite back up the tree and they watched the raiders depart, all carrying nuts in their mouths.

An hour later the Greys were back, collecting more of the Reds' precious Harvest, not even leaving the sacrosanct eighth nut as required by the Kernel:

One out of eight nuts
Must be left to germinate.
Here grows our future.

Alder was on the trunk, raging at the Greys, when Marguerite noticed a Red whom she recognised as the father of Chip. He was directing the foraging party. She slipped away through the branches and came down behind him.

"What's going on?" she asked angrily. "Those are our reserves!"

Crag turned to her scornfully. "You deserve to have nothing. You are all blasphemers, story-tellers and pleasure-indulgers – you don't even collect metal! And you've corrupted my son!' he added, venom in his voice. "At least these nuts will feed Sun-fearing squirrels even if they are grey. If you get your lot to repent and help us fill the Temple, I will consider sharing this bounty with you."

"That bounty, as you call it, is *ours*," Marguerite retorted. Then, noticing that Crag was looking over her shoulder, she turned to see that there was a group of Greys close behind her.

"Shall we remove her, Temple Masster?" asked a grey female with a broken tooth.

"She's just leaving," Crag replied, as Marguerite leapt for the tree-trunk. "Carry on collecting the bounty. Don't talk to the Blasphemers."

Marguerite re-joined her family and companions, and

told them what had occurred. When she had finished, Chip slipped away to speak to his father. He found him as Marguerite had, organising the Greys and directing their plundering.

"Father," he said hesitantly, "these are nice squirrels. They are what they call 'friendly', and they *do* respect the Sun, only in a different way from us. Why don't you talk more with them?"

Crag glowered at him. "They really have got you in their paws, haven't they? You always were weak. Well, they won't have you much longer!" He nodded to two Greys who had come up behind Chip, and they seized his forelimbs and dragged him, scratching and chattering in fear and anger, towards the North-east Wood.

Tansy had trailed Chip, or Chipling as she usually called him, when he had gone to speak to his father, and had seen him being taken away by the two Greys. She was annoyed because Marguerite, though always agreeing that they must take the Woodstock to Ourland, appeared to be doing nothing about it. She had vague hopes that Chip might, in some way, be able to help her. Tansy followed them quietly, through the treetops, wondering what it was that one of the Greys had said to the youngster that made him stop calling out. Crag and the laden Greys were coming along the ground below her in a group, hampered by their loads of nuts.

When in sight of the Temple Tree she stopped, hid herself and watched what was happening. She saw Rusty run down the trunk and across the ground, hug her skinny son to her and then, seeing Crag approaching, push Chip away and begin to scold him unconvincingly. "Why did you go away with those Blasphemers?" she asked. "Your father and I were most upset. Come on into the Temple and repent for your sins."

Chip, now alert to such things, had detected a note of warmth in her voice and followed her meekly.

As he went he heard his father issuing instructions to the Greys that "the chit" was to be watched at all times. The broken-toothed female appointed guards.

Inside the Temple Chip could see that there was much more metal than when he had last been here; the main trunk was nearly full and the hollow secondary trunk, which grew away from the main tree like a squirrel's tail from its body, was also being filled. There were many more Greys too; others must have arrived from the north. They were all busy, either bringing in metal or stowing the plundered nuts in the hollows and crevices of upper limbs. Ivy offered him a nut, but he refused it.

Later, when it was dark and Crag had said the familiar words of the Evening Prayer, Chip tried to slip away, but every exit was blocked by an alert grey squirrel.

He sought out his mother's sleeping place and tried to join her, but she pushed him away. He could sense his father's disapproval.

"None of your blasphemous behaviour here. This is a Temple of the Sun," the harsh voice came out of the darkness. Chip went back to his sleeping place and lay there, rigid and cold, thinking of the warmth of his friends' dreys. He yearned to feel Tansywistful's warm body snug against his.

*

Tansy was awake, wondering what her young friend was doing. She knew from her own experience and from Chip's descriptions just how it would be in the Temple Tree. She tried to think of some way of getting him back. In the morning she would have another look at the Temple Tree, if she could avoid Crag and the Greys. As she lay there, thoughts of her family and her friends on Ourland crept up on her and she again felt an agonising guilt that she had not been able to do more to get help to them. There was nothing *she* could do, she told herself, unless Marguerite and the others could be persuaded to assist her. In the meantime that funny youngster needed her.

Eventually she fell asleep, to awake in the darkness, overcome by marten-dread, and she lay shivering until dawn.

Neither Spindle nor Wood Anemone had slept, each sure that their indiscretion had resulted in the raid by the Greys, but neither could speak of it to the other.

Marguerite was trying to find some way of reconciling her desire to help Tansy with her duty as a parent and as Tagger to the Blue Pool community. She had discussed her dilemma with her friend Dandelion, who told her that her life-mate, Alder the Leader, was adamant that Marguerite must put her duty to the community first. He had led them all to the Blue Pool and they needed to stay together as a strong unit, especially as there was now an obvious threat from the unpredictable Greys and the strange Red, Crag. Should she insist on a Council Meeting to discuss it all openly?

The following morning was clear and bright, with frost

crystals sparkling on the pine needles as Tansy slipped quietly through the branches towards the Temple Tree. A party of Greys passed under her, noisily heading for the pool and more "bounty". She crouched on a high branch until they were out of sight, then went on even more cautiously.

Greys were leaving the Temple Tree, each group heading in a different direction. These, she assumed, were metal-hunting parties.

When she reached a pine tree where she could overlook the clearing in which the Temple Tree stood, she could see that some Greys had been left on guard. Seven or eight of the biggest were either patrolling the ground near the tree or were in an upright and alert stance close to the entrances to the hollow. She settled down in a dense clump of pine needles to watch.

As the sun got higher, the patrolling by the Greys slowed down, but she saw the activity intensify when Crag the Temple Master appeared at one of the holes and came down the trunk, followed by even more Greys. They left, heading eastwards, Crag dominating the larger and more powerful grey squirrels. Another party left, heading north, led by the broken-toothed female.

Tansy continued her silent watch.

It was nearly High Sun and several parties of Greys had come and gone when she saw Chip emerge from the highest of the holes in the Temple Tree, with a red female that she knew must be his mother. She watched as the two climbed one of the spiky dead top branches of the stag-headed oak. They clung there, whispering to one another.

Tansy in the pine and the Greys on the ground were

watching them and listening, trying to overhear what was being said, but Chip and Rusty kept their voices low.

"Your father will be furious if he knows that we have been talking like this," Rusty whispered, looking fearfully down at the patrolling squirrels.

"That's just what I mean. We can't live our entire lives in fear of what Crag-Pa will say."

"But if we don't do as he says, it will be the Sunless Pit for us both – for ever."

"Do you really believe there is such a place?" Chip asked. "Tansywistful doesn't. She says it was invented in the old days by the 'Nobles' to make lesser squirrels obey them."

"How would she know?" Rusty asked. "She's only a young squirrel herself." She was about to tell her son about the dreadful night and the day of darkness when he interrupted.

"At the Blue Pool they – we – they – all discuss things, you can say anything you want to and the others will listen to what you say and tell you *their* ideas. It's ever so interesting. Everything is shared."

"What does 'shared' mean?" Rusty asked, keeping a watchful eye for Crag's return, hoping he wouldn't come back for a while.

Chip explained this concept as best he could, then tried to explain "Love".

"All the squirrels 'love' one another. They help each other whenever they can. Even when they disagree about something and quarrel, they soon make it up because they don't like seeing their friends upset." He then had to explain "friends" to a puzzled Rusty.

"But what about sins?" she asked.

"They don't have them. All the things that Crag-Pa calls sins they do all the time, and they don't feel bad about them." He described snugging up and comfort and warmth to his increasingly perturbed mother.

"Don't you think that their way seems more natural?" Chip asked.

"I don't know about this 'natural'. We've *always* done things the way your father told us to." However, she let her mind relax enough to remember the feeling of warmth and rightness she'd had when she'd cuddled her young son when he was a dreyling, so long, long ago.

"What about these untrue stories that they tell, that upset your father so?" she asked, after looking round the clearing again.

"Tansywistful says that stories don't have to be true as long as every squirrel knows them to be 'stories'. They are sometimes just for fun and sometimes they have messages in them which you have to work out." He tried to explain "fun".

"We'd better go down," Rusty said. "Your father will be back soon."

Entering the hollow of the tree by the highest hole, Rusty allowed her paw to rest momentarily on her son's shoulder. He was right, it did feel natural.

Tansy, across the clearing, watched them go in out of her sight, waited a little while longer and then went back to the Blue Pool.

Chapter 21

Old Oak was feeling nauseous. There was an overwhelming scent of decay filling the Bunker. Each squirrel knew that it came from the decaying body of Fern, buried in the powdery punkwood at the back of the hollow, but, out of respect for Oak's feelings, none had openly remarked on it. Now, with the temperature rising whenever sunshine heated the hollow tree, it could no longer be ignored. Oak called a Council Meeting.

"My fellow squirrels," he began, "we have been through much hardship and danger together and I have valued your support. Now, though, since my life-mate Fern has gone Sunwards, I am increasingly feeling my age and do not believe that I can give the leadership you all deserve."

He paused and there was a murmur of concern from the others.

"We are virtually out of food, the air in the Bunker is getting sour and soon we will have to leave, despite the danger from the marten outside. I just don't feel up to taking the responsibility of leading you; my brain is tired and I can no longer think as clearly as I used to. I propose to stand down and help you to select a new Council

Leader." He slumped back, exhausted by the strain of this long speech and the relief of having at last given up what had become an impossible burden to him.

The squirrels waited. There were no real precedents for a Leader standing down. Clover the Carer and Tagger fumbled in her mind for a Kernel to help guide them. All she found was:

In any crisis
A Leader's first duty is –
To keep hope alive.

But this did not seem appropriate, though the need to keep hope alive was apparent enough. Could I be Leader? she asked herself, then dismissed the idea. It was hard enough combining the duties of Tagger and Carer. She was training the two ex-princesses Voxglove and Cowzlip to take over the Caring role and they were learning fast, but it would be a long time before she could let them carry on without her help.

She looked around at the assembled squirrels sitting expectantly in the dim light waiting for someone to propose something.

Chestnut the Doubter for Leader? she wondered. If they appointed him, he wouldn't believe it and his attitude was always negative anyway. A Leader must be positive!

His life-mate Heather Treetops? She would like the honour, as she always boasted that her ancestors were noble squirrels, but she had never shown real depth and, though prepared to criticise others, she had few ideas of her own.

What about her own life-mate Larch the Curious? She smiled to herself. Fond as she was of him, he was far too impetuous, and his insatiable curiosity often overtook caution. That wouldn't do in a Leader.

She ran her eye round the circle of squirrels, dismissing the ex-zervantz; they had little concept of action other than doing what they were told.

Ex-prince Fir was sickly, probably as a result of the inbreeding of the Royal family, but Just Poplar looked strong enough. Of course. He was the natural choice!

Without further hesitation Clover said, "I propose Just Poplar to be our new Leader."

Poplar looked uncomfortable and said, "It's lezz than a year zinze uz became King and uz gave that up at wonz, not liking the thingz uz would have to do. Uz don't think that uz'z a zuitable zquirrel to be a Leader."

Each squirrel remembered how Poplar had abdicated and given up all his titles, privileges and duties to become Just Poplar and how relaxed he had seemed after that. But then they thought how helpful and friendly he had been to every squirrel since then and his Royal background still gave him an air of authority. Looking at each other, they seemed to decide, as one, that he *would* make an excellent new Leader and there was a clamour of approval.

"Poplar for Leader, Poplar, Poplar."

One of the ex-zervantz called, "Long live King Poplar", but was glowered into silence by the others.

After listening to the acclaim, Poplar raised his tail. "If it iz the wizh of yew all, then uz acceptz. However, there will be no talk of "King" Poplar. Uz do not care for titles, uz do not even want a tag other than the won uz have been comfortable with. Uz'll only agree if uz can continue to be 'Juzt Poplar'."

A little forest of raised tails indicated unanimous acceptance.

Clover breathed a sigh of relief and Old Oak slumped further as he felt the burden he had carried for so long transfer to younger shoulders.

"Uz muzt make planz," Just Poplar announced, and, as Oak moved out of the Leader's place, he moved across to occupy it.

Peafowl, peafowl, peafowl! Blood was sick of peafowl. There were only eight females left now, plus the big old cock bird with the long tail. I must go and find a squirrel, or at least a rabbit, he thought. He was still puzzled by the mysterious disappearance of the squirrels. Occasionally he caught a whiff of squirrel-scent on the breeze, but never enough for him to track down their hiding place.

He came out of the church into the brightness, blinked and looked about him. Despite the sunshine, he knew that winter was not yet over and that snow and bitter winds could return at any time. Honeysuckle leaves were showing bright green, but no other new vegetation had yet dared to emerge. He climbed a bare-branched oak-tree and scented the air. Ducks and sea-birds in the lagoon; that fishy scent was probably from the cormorants who were drying their outspread wings in the sunshine. No – he wanted mammal-meat today. Even a mouse would be welcome. Two mice, or three, would be better still.

Blood leapt from tree to tree above the swamp, watching the ground but not following any particular route, then, thinking that he was more likely to find live, warm-blooded mammals away from the bog-pools, he turned southwards towards the neglected and overgrown fields. It would have to be rabbit; some would be out in the open today.

He stopped suddenly, just as he was about to leap for the next tree. Squirrel-scent was rising from below to tickle his nostrils and make his mouth water. He clung to the branch testing the air. This was not normal squirrel-scent; this was dead squirrel-scent, long-dead squirrel-scent. He went slowly down the trunk.

Below him was a willow tree that leaned out over a pool of dark water and mud. He dropped on to the sloping trunk. The scent was stronger now and there was a touch of live squirrel in it – not fresh, a few days old at least. He prowled along the trunk, scratching at the bark and sniffing. Where *was* that scent coming from? There were no holes visible and yet the scent was clearly coming from inside. It must be hollow. He went to the foot of the tree and looked up. There was a hole on the underside, above the water and mud. So that was where the squirrels had been hiding for so long! No wonder he hadn't found them.

The stench of dead squirrel was pouring from the hole, turning his stomach and drowning any live squirrel smells that might be about. None could be in the tree now, so where had they gone? Nose down, he began to sniff about in ever widening circles.

Chapter 22

Tansy was doubly worried. Already sick with concern for her family under threat from the pine marten over on Ourland, now her young friend Chipling was being held against his will by Crag and the Greys of the Second Wave.

How could she help him escape? Marguerite, Alder and the other senior squirrels were now totally absorbed in the problem of finding food. All their reserves and even the Sun-tithe nuts had been scented out, dug up and carried away by the Greys. Her friends had little thought to spare for Chip, who at least was unlikely to starve, and, it seemed, even less thought for the Ourlanders under threat from the pine marten.

Tansy slipped away through the treetops to the hiding place from where she could watch the Temple Tree. She could see Chip on one of the dead top-branches talking to his mother again. They sat a little apart from one another, not as close as normal Reds would be when talking within families, but they didn't appear quite as stiff as they had been before.

Several Greys patrolled the ground below, occasionally

glancing up at the two Reds in the high branches. Tansy wondered what Rusty and Chip were saying to each other.

Rusty had given up "trying to talk some sense into her son", as Crag had directed her to do, though she sinfully lied to him each evening that she had tried her best. She looked forward to hearing more and more about life in the Blue Pool community from the youngster. She had heard all the Acorn stories that her son could remember, and he was now teaching her the Kernels that he had learned. Today he had got to the Mating Kernel:

Mating is a joy
Sun-given to squirrel folk
To make more squirrels.

"Tansywistful told me all about it. Fun, and chases through the trees and then joining together with your favourite. Did you do it on Portland?"

"Yes," said Rusty, hesitantly, "sort of. But not quite like you say," she added, recalling the brief, cold act with Crag, once a year in the darkness of the cave. "Yes – sort of."

A thought struck her. "Have you and Tansy – you know – have you and Tansy. . . ?" She could not use the word; it had implications of dreadful sinning and the Sunless Pit.

"Not yet, but I would like to, if she chooses me. But she's not of my year and may prefer another squirrel." He thought a little jealously of Tamarisk the Forthright, and shuddered to think of Tansywistful being pursued joyously through the trees by "the Mouth" whilst he, Chip, who loved her so much, was trapped here, guarded by foreign Greys.

The two of them sat on the dead branch, each silent with their musings, Chip staring vacantly across the clearing.

A red tail flicked momentarily in the tree opposite. Or did it? He focused his eyes and raised his tail slowly. The tail opposite flicked again. Chip quickly looked down, fearful that the Greys might have seen what he had, but the patrolling continued as before. He lowered his tail and raised it. Again an answering flick. It could only be Tansy – his Tansywistful – come to see that he was all right. His heart swelled in his chest and he dug his claws deep into the soft wood of the dead branch.

Tansywistful had come!

Tansy knew that Chip had seen her, but she was powerless to do anything other than watch, and occasionally, when she judged it safe to do so, flick a signal with her tail.

After a while she made the "farewell" signal, waited for the half-concealed acknowledgement, then went back through the treetops to the Blue Pool Demesne, her mind full of impossible rescue ideas.

Rusty and Chip went down and into the hollow of the Temple Tree, their bodies in comforting contact as they squeezed through the hole together.

Just Poplar was not sure if he had done the right thing. True, he had brought the entire group safely from the now uninhabitable Bunker to *this* place, but was this a safe place for them to be? He looked out from the round end of a broken drainpipe and could see Heather and Cowzlip on guard down on the shore, their backs to the sea, watching the trees and bushes on the bank behind him. Once, though he did not know this, a pottery factory had stood on this site and the many broken and badly fired drainpipes and chimney pots had been thrown on to scrap-piles on the foreshore.

In the seventy-five years since the factory had closed and the pipemakers had given up and moved away, the wind had blown sand, soil and leaves in and over the pipe-shards until little remained visible on the surface. Pines and birches had colonised the new ground, growing from tiny seedlings to mature trees with their roots reaching down through and past the broken pipes, many of which were now deep underground.

In this hidden labyrinth the young Prince Poplar, as he had been then, had played hide and seek with his brothers, sisters, cousins and the dreylings of the zervantz until they knew every passageway and dead-end intimately.

In the last two days since he had led his party here he had insisted that every squirrel learn the layout, and know of each exit hole and how to find their way about, even in darkness. At first he had taken them personally through all the passages, then had encouraged games which would last for hours, before he let a few at a time out amongst the bushes and trees of the bank to forage, watched over by alert pickets.

As Just Poplar was about to turn back into the drainpipe, he saw one of these pickets, Heather Treetops, stand to her full height and peer up the bank, her tail moving slowly from left to right and back. It was the "possible danger" signal.

Poplar thought quickly. There were no foraging parties out at present, thank the Sun; the squirrels underground were resting after the last game and only the two guards were outside.

Heather was standing, then crouching, in an attempt to identify something, and the other picket, Cowzlip, was moving closer to her, staring in the same direction. The tails of both were now moving swiftly from side to side. Poplar turned round and called, "Danger", his voice sounding oddly magnified in the smooth glazed pipe. The murmur of voices in the darkness behind him ceased. Then Heather and Cowzlip came bounding across the ground to join him in the tunnel entrance. "It's the marten," Heather said breathlessly. "He's found us."

Blood paused at the top of the bank, savouring the fresh squirrel-scent all about him. He had seen the two on the shore and had watched them disappear underground. He *would* have squirrel today! He padded down the bank, then out on to the edge of the beach, aware that he was being watched. His feet crunched on dry black seaweed and old crab-shells.

He picked a crab-shell up and tossed it in the air. There was no hurry now. He crouched and studied the bank. Holes everywhere, very round and unnatural-looking, but he let his imagination wander. A squirrel in each – just waiting for him to take his pick.

Saliva dribbled from the corner of his mouth as he went up to the first hole and peered inside. He paused there, waiting for his night-vision to come as his pupils enlarged in the dim light. He could hear movement deep in the bank ahead and waves of delicious squirrel-scent wafted out past him. He was sure that he could see the end of a reddy-brown tail and he went into the opening, his claws scratching on the smooth brown glaze of the pipe which sloped slightly uphill away from him. The tail disappeared around a corner and he followed it; the squirrel was always just out of sight, except for tantalising tail-tip glimpses every now and then. Passages that he was sure would contain a squrriel ended abruptly in a mass of roots, or opened on to the beach, and he had to allow his eyes to readjust again after turning back into the dim light of the labyrinth. There were callings and whisperings down every passage and pipe, but he could never see more of any squirrel than that elusive tail-tip.

Blood knew by the scent-changes that his quarry was being switched as one grew tired and another took over, but no matter how hard he tried or how fast he ran, the tempting squirrels were always one corner ahead. After what seemed like hours he was dizzy and tired. Mocking squirrel voices came to his ears from above, below and behind him, and glimpses of red tails flashing in side-passages invited him to turn and chase them, yet never once did he actually get within touching distance of any squirrel.

He was worn out, hungry and, most of all, frustrated. Finally he left the labyrinth at the first open hole he came to and padded off down the beach, glaring back at the open ends of the pipes. It would have to be rabbit today, but tomorrow would be squirrel, definitely squirrel, without any shadow of a doubt – squirrel!

Chapter 23

"I'm sure that he wants to be back with us," Tansy was telling the Blue Pool Council. "He told me a good deal about what it was like at the Temple Tree before he came to us, and I've seen it myself. Why else would the Greys be keeping guard? They definitely seemed to be there to stop Chipling – Chip – from leaving. I could tell by the way they were watching him. They are *not* honouring the Kernel:

Squirrels must be free
To come and go as they please.
None may be constrained.

She looked round for confirmation.

Marguerite agreed. 'If he is being held unwillingly, then we *must* release him.' Others signalled agreement.

Alder said, "I'll go and talk to that Crag – what does he call himself? – the Temple Master."

It was decided that Alder and Marguerite would go, but that Juniper, Tamarisk and Tansy would follow and stay within calling distance in case there was any trouble. Rowan the Bold, now a respectable father, though still loving action of any kind was, to his disappointment, left in charge of the remaining squirrels and the youngsters.

The party separated into two groups as they approached the Temple Tree, Marguerite and Alder arriving in the clearing just as Crag returned with a party of Greys who were dragging a length of rusty chain between them.

Crag surveyed the Reds coldly. "What are two Blasphemers doing at my Temple?" he asked. "Come to repent for your many sins?"

"We have come to check that your youngster is not being held against his will," Alder replied.

"My son is *my* business," Crag snapped back. "Now, away. I don't want you corrupting these repentant silver-furred servants of the Sun. Away with you both."

The Temple Master turned to direct the grim-faced Greys as they dragged the chain up the trunk to an upper hole. Alder and Marguerite heard it rattle down inside the tree behind them as they re-entered the woodland.

"What happened?" Tansy asked eagerly.

Marguerite told her as they went back to the pool together, discussing what options were now open to them.

"Use the New Woodstock," said Tamarisk. "Curl their whiskers up – they deserve it!"

Tansy had never experienced the full range of the Woodstock's power. Tamarisk explained how different numbers scratched on it after the X had varying effects, from a painful 2, and a whisker-curling 3 or 4, to a killing 6 or 7.

The original Woodstock, he told her, had been

exhausted in destroying the Power Square, but a second one had been found and hidden for possible future need. Perhaps the time had come to use it.

They discussed the points for and against.

"It does give us an advantage," Alder said. "They are bigger and stronger than us, and it was one of their kind who broke my tail." There was a measure of savagery in his voice.

"But it wasn't these actual ones," replied Marguerite, and she quoted the Focus Kernel:

The errant squirrel
Should be punished. Do not harm
Its friends, nor its kin.

"The Greys are all the same," said Tamarisk. "They hate us Reds. Look how they treated Bluebell – they killed her!"

Marguerite glanced at her life-mate, Juniper. Bluebell had been his first life-mate, but she had died while warning other Reds of an imminent Grey attack. Juniper looked as if he would like to take on all Greys himself, with or without a Woodstock.

"We don't know if there is any force left in the New Woodstock," she reminded them.

"We could try it out on Juniper," Tamarisk said mischievously, remembering that it was Juniper who had first experienced the whisker-curling effect of the Woodstock's force.

"Not on your nutpile," said Juniper. "Clover had to bite my whiskers off before my head stopped spinning and it was weeks before I could think clearly or even climb a tree! You're not trying it out on me!"

The mention of nutpiles reminded Marguerite of the acute food shortage which was now following the plundering of their reserves by the Greys. Each time they saw Crag he seemed to have more and more Greys at his command. They must be flooding in from the north and east, part of the Second Wave. Marguerite was regretting her decision to treat them so suspiciously in the autumn and send them to the Lightning Tree area for the winter. But, as she told herself, at that time they hadn't known that Crag and his family were there.

Looking behind you
There is never any mist,
The view is superb.

They had to deal with the situation as it was now. They had little food, a young Red was being held against his will *and* against the ancient Kernel Lore, the land was being overrun by Greys of the Second Wave, all seemingly under the influence of the Temple Master, and on top of all this, Tansy was constantly pressing her to go to the aid of the squirrels on Ourland. So many things to be considered and no clear line of action to be seen.

They had reached the edge of the hollow in which the Blue Pool lay. The surface was calm in the late-winter sunshine and the upside-down reflections of the Beachend trees were green against the blue of the mirrored sky. Even in her agitated state Marguerite felt the surge of joy that always came when she looked at the loveliness of the pool and its setting. The Sun forbid that she would ever have to leave it again. Yet somehow she knew it would come to that.

Chapter 24

It was a night for dreaming.

Crag dreamed of the day when both trunks of the Temple Tree would be filled with metal, safely stowed there to prove to the Sun that he was a *worthy squirrel.* No Sunless Pit for him! The hollows were filling fast; every day more Greys arrived and were instructed by Ivy that this was the local custom and therefore, in accordance with their instructions from the Oval Drey at Woburn, must be followed. She was also adept at describing the Sunless Pit to the newcomers; he could not do better himself.

A few feet from him Rusty, on a ledge in the cold hollow of the Temple Tree, dreamed of loving and cuddling, then awoke shivering with fear, afraid that Crag might somehow know of her sinful dreams.

Chip, in a hollow lower down in the tree, was also dreaming of loving and cuddling, but with no such sense of sinfulness.

The object of his dreams, Tansywistful, in the drey above the pool, was dreaming of a pine marten eating her family one by one, whilst she watched helplessly from a tree surrounded by water.

On the island the object of her dream, Blood, had returned from his unsuccessful hunt in the pottery labyrinth to find the church door shut and neither sight nor sound of the peacock and the peahens. There had been a tangle of human-scents around the church, and some of the undergrowth that had been invading the building and its surrounds had been cut back. He had found a dry place under a rhododendron bush nearby, and now slept and dreamed of the peacock. His pride prevented him from dreaming of squirrels that night.

Mogul, the peacock, was at that time crouched uneasily on a beam in an unfamiliar shed, the remainder of his harem of peahens perched alongside him, their heads under their wings. In his restless slumber he was resenting the way he had been shooed out of the stone building that had been their home for so long by a party of humans who had come into the church and started to clean it up after many years of abandonment and neglect.

Mogul's dream was that, when spring came, he would dazzle his hens and all the humans with a display of colour such as none of them had ever seen before. He would especially show off to that man in the brown and green clothes, the man with the picture of the oak-leaves and the acorns on his chest, who was clearly the Cock of the parties of men now busy all across the island.

The object of Mogul's dreams was the National Trust Head Warden, who had recently been appointed when the Trust had taken over Brownsea Island. He was dreaming of – or perhaps it would be more honest to say, lying awake worrying about – all the things that had to be organised and carried out before the official opening ceremony, scheduled for late May.

Apart from the church, the restoration of which was being carried out by a group of volunteers from a mainland parish, there were countless things to be done. Masses of the rhododendrons had to be cleared, buildings would have to be repaired and a power line brought over from the mainland. The diesel generator was just not adequate. So much to do, so little time! Some people just don't realise *how* much; all they kept asking him was "Are the squirrels still there?" Come to think of it, he hadn't seen them for a while. Finally he fell asleep with pictures of squirrels filling his dreams.

Not many of the Ourland squirrels were asleep. Just Poplar, fearful of a return visit from the marten, had employed another trick from his dreyling-hood games. An hour before high-tide he had led the entire party out of the labyrinth on to the shore and they had set off in the dusk, along the beach below the high-water mark. Soon the rising tide would obliterate their tracks and their scent, so it would appear that they had all vanished into the sea! They had left the beach after rounding the point and were now resting uneasily in the darkness near the ruined Man-dreys of Maryland at the extreme western end of Ourland.

Old Oak was asleep. The burden of leadership lifted from him by Just Poplar, Oak seemed to be shrinking in on himself, sleeping often, and little concerned with the events going on around him. Earlier that day he had led the youngsters out of the rear entrance of the labyrinth as the marten had gone in at the front, and had kept them amused whilst the other mature squirrels had confused and demoralised the hunter. Then there had been that long trek over the sand and the pebbles of the beach. His age now excused him from guard duty, so he slept and dreamed of his daughter, Marguerite the Bright One, and his son, Rowan the Bold. What a character *he* was, totally fearless. He would have *enjoyed* today – fooling that marten!

Rowan himself, snug in his drey at the Humanside Guardianship of the Blue Pool, cuddled up to his life-mate, Meadowsweet, tagged Rowan's Love, and their dreyling, Young Bluebell. Rowan was dreaming of the day his sister, Marguerite, had shown him the numbers she had invented for counting things. The odd-shaped figures paraded across the backs of his eyelids – 1 Z 3 4 5 6 7 — 10 11 1Z Each had the right number of corners to hide nuts in, as Marguerite had explained, after she had scratched the figures in the clay. 1 had one corner, Z had two and so on. Neither of them had dreamed then of the power these numbers would have when scratched on to the smooth surface of the Woodstock.

The Woodstock itself was the object of Marguerite's dreams. She dreamed that she was pointing it at Crag and threatening to curl his whiskers if he did not hand over Young Chip, and stop this business of misleading the gullible Greys.

Juniper stirred next to her, briefly waking Young Oak and Young Burdock who, after wriggling about and nudging one another, dropped off to sleep again, leaving Marguerite awake in the darkness.

She was not sure now if she was dreaming or not. Images tumbled through her mind. At first she felt surrounded by a thick grey mist filled with a hidden menace. Then a shaft of sunlight broke through and in its light she could see the long sweep of a pebble beach as it had once been described to her by Chip. Dandelion had portrayed it again in the Whale story. It was there that the second wave had swept Primrose out to join Acorn in the water before the whale had taken them to safety on Ourland. The Second Wave – that was what the Greys called themselves now.

Did this mean that the Greys were destined to sweep the Reds off the Mainland to Ourland? She tensed, then relaxed to let her subconscious thoughts rise to the surface like cones dropped in a pool. The first picture to come was of the great ruined Man-drey that the squirrels could see in the distance from the tops of the poolside trees on clear days. In her mind a rainbow arched through the sky over the heath, bright against the dark sky beyond. One end appeared to be on the Lightning Tree and the other on the ruined Man-drey.

Before she could interpret this, another picture emerged. She could see a huge slab of stone tilted on its edge and seemingly balanced on other smaller stones beneath. It was surrounded by desolate heathland, but in the distance beyond it was the sea. The rainbow came again, faint and nebulous at first, then glowing brighter and brighter as the sun broke through the grey clouds that massed behind her. Now one end of the rainbow was on the great stone and the other far out to sea. She followed the arch with her imagination and where it ended she could see three black dolphins curving gracefully through the waves. She remembered Malin and Lundy, the dolphins who had helped her when, with Juniper, Spindle and Wood Anemone, she had been carried out to sea in a rubber boat the previous year.

She felt that the two larger dolphins were these same ones and that they were trying to communicate with her. She strained all her senses to try to pick up the silent thought-waves, but the picture faded and she woke feeling sick and empty.

At first light Marguerite slipped out of the warm drey and ran through the mist-wreathed treetops to the drey of Alder and Dandelion. She paused outside and whispered the Calling Kernel:

Hello and greetings.
I visit you and bring peace.
Emerge or I leave.

Dandelion's sleepy voice responded, "Marguerite, come on in. It'll be a bit crowded, but you're always welcome. Do you have news?"

"I must speak quietly to Alder. Is he awake?"

"I'll come out now," Alder called, and emerged, blinking, into the cold air.

Marguerite, as always when she first saw him each day, had to adjust to the fact that he had no tail, and remind herself that this did not mean that he had no brain. In fact, he had proved to be an excellent Leader, though perhaps a little lacking in imagination. She smiled to herself as she remembered what Dandelion had once said to her: that she, Marguerite, had enough imagination for three ordinary squirrels, and some to spare!

They brushed whiskers on the grooming branch, then Marguerite signalled Alder to follow her out of ear-twitch of the drey's other occupants. "I don't want to alarm any squirrel, but last night I had the strangest dream."

Alder looked puzzled, and waited for Marguerite to continue.

"I don't know even if it was a dream; it seemed far stronger than any dream I have ever had before."

"Tell me about it," said Alder gently, seeing how agitated Marguerite was.

She told Alder what she had seen in the night. As she did so, the pictures strengthened in her mind and she became more and more convinced that they were more than just a dream.

Alder asked her to repeat what she had told him to Dandelion, his life-mate.

When Marguerite got to the great rock set in the desolate heathland, Dandelion broke in. "That is an exact description of the Agglestone that my grandfather told me about. It is on the heath between the ruined Man-drey and the sea. He described it to me once. He found it when he was on climbabout as a youngster and slept the night on the top of it. You've had a Sun-scene."

"What's a Sun-scene?" asked Marguerite, the term new to her.

"Do you remember my telling you about the Bard we used to have back at our home near the Barrow of the Wolves? He used to have Sun-scenes. It happened when the Sun wanted to tell us something or warn us of danger. He had a Sun-scene before the Silver Tide came, but we didn't really believe it and that's why Alder lost his tail. You must be gifted like our Bard was.

"We shall have to leave here and head for Ourland.

That's the message for us. Remember the second wave of the Whale story? That ended happily there for Acorn and Primrose."

Marguerite looked at Dandelion. Was she mixing her stories with reality, or were there really Sun-scenes sent to receptive squirrels? It would solve the problem of Tansy wanting her to take the Woodstock to Ourland and yet . . . She looked down on the winter blue of the pool. It would be unlikely that she would ever see that again if they did leave, but they had no food reserves, and who knew what the Greys might do next.

"We must have a Council Meeting," she said. "This morning."

Chapter 25

At the meeting the squirrels discussed Marguerite's Sun-scene and what it would mean for them all. Demoralised after losing their food reserves and ever conscious of the nearness of the Greys and the zealous Crag, there was no resistance to the proposal to move away to the ruined Man-drey, though they all regretted having to leave their beautiful home.

Alder quoted the Acceptance Kernel:

If it hurts too much
Thinking of what cannot be,
Put it out of mind.

"Who knows the best way to get to the ruined Man-drey?" he asked.

"I do," said Rowan. "I went near there when I was on climbabout. There is a great mound in a gap in the hills with towers of stone on top. Humans used to live there, but now they live in smaller Man-dreys on the other side of the mound."

Dandelion said, "That's what they call a castle. Or so my grandfather used to say."

"There's an easy way to go there," said Rowan.

"Through the woods to the east are two metal 'lines' that go right to the Man-dreys by this 'castle' thing. I followed them when I was on climbabout. Easy travel, no swamps or wide streams to cross, but you're on the ground all the time, so you have to be alert."

"I remember crossing those lines last time we had to leave here," Juniper said, "on the way to Ourland. What are they for?" He looked at Dandelion.

"Sun knows. The humans must have made them, but why, I don't know."

Tansy signalled a request to speak. "I know that I have been urging you all to do something about helping to save the Ourland squirrels from the pine marten, and if we are all going, then we surely must take the Woodstock." She paused and the others nodded agreement.

"But before we go, we must also do something about Chipling. He is still being held against his will, contrary to the Freedom Kernel. I propose that we first work out a plan to free him so that he can come with us – if that is his wish."

Tamarisk glowered at her, then turned away as she scowled back.

Alder spoke. "Tansy is right. We cannot leave the youngster like that. Suggestions, please. Then when he is safe, we'll follow those metal lines. We'll need to travel fast, once we've rescued Chip. It'll be like poking a stick in a wasps' nest."

The rescue party approached the tree stealthily so as not to alert the guarding Greys.

The rest of the community had left the Blue Pool, dragging the Woodstock with them, to circle round and cross open country to the south and east until they came to the metal lines. Then they were to follow these towards the castle mound as fast as they could, their speed dependent on the youngsters in the party. Alder was in charge, and they had left before High Sun to gain maximum distance before nightfall.

Marguerite was leading the rescuers; her party consisted of Rowan the Bold, delighted at the prospect of action, Tansy the Wistful and Tamarisk the Forthright. Tamarisk had continued to be unenthusiastic about the need for rescuing Chip at all, but had not spoken against the plan, as Tansy was so obviously in favour.

Now he was rearguard on a highly dangerous mission. At least he might be able to protect Tansy and persuade bossy Marguerite to withdraw if it got too risky!

They climbed the tree which Tansy had been in when she signalled, and saw that Chip and his mother were sitting out on the dead branch, as they did on most days after High Sun. Watching the Greys, Tansy flicked her tail. Chip responded at once. He must have been watching for her, Tamarisk thought jealously.

Tansy was making pointing-signals with her paws, and Chip was sitting up and staring across the clearing. Stupid brat, thought Tamarisk, and was relieved when Chip responded to a signal from Tansy to appear relaxed. Then Rusty sat up and stared until Chip whispered urgently to her. Tamarisk looked down, but the guards were chatting amongst themselves, apparently unaware of anything happening above their heads.

Rusty was the unknown part of their plan. If they were successful, she might come away with Chip, or she might just turn a blind eye as he went off with them. They had all agreed that, as his mother, she was unlikely to do anything to alert the guards or to prevent his escape, but no squirrel could be *sure* when these Portlanders, with their strange customs, were involved.

Marguerite moved quietly through the treetops to the north side of the clearing as they had planned earlier, and dropped a cone to the ground. The Greys, instantly alert, sat up and looked in that direction. Keeping out of sight, Marguerite dropped another cone. The Greys moved forward slowly to investigate, all their attention focused on the north side of the glade.

Tansy flicked an unmistakable "go down and head that way" signal to Chip, holding a paw to her mouth to indicate the need for silence. Tamarisk saw Chip whisper to his mother as though trying to persuade her to come with him, but she shook her head, touched him on the shoulder and watched as he slipped down the far side of the trunk.

Marguerite dropped a larger cone and the Grey guards moved forward, trying to see what was happening. They chattered to one another, all peering in the direction of the sound.

Tamarisk and Tansy moved through the treetops, silently, to circle round and meet Chip.

As they were doing this, Rusty broke off a piece of rotten bark and let it fall from the Temple Tree, causing the nervous Greys to turn and stare up at her. Marguerite dropped another cone and the Greys ran in her direction only to turn again as Rusty called down something that the Reds, now busy withdrawing, could not make out. The Greys too seemed puzzled and sat staring upwards and trying to hear what she was saying, but somehow the words were not clear from the ground. One Grey shouted up to her to speak louder.

Tansy and Tamarisk had, by now, joined a breathless Chip and were heading for the railway line, where they waited and watched from a line-side tree until Marguerite came into sight, skipping along between the rails triumphantly. They all embraced silently. There were no sounds of pursuit.

Congratulating each other on the success of their plan, they hurried along the track, Tamarisk and Chip vying with each other to be nearest Tansy, until they caught up with the party of tired and anxious squirrels where the humans' roadway crossed over their railway on a bridge. Marguerite, checking that Juniper had the Woodstock with him, was intrigued to see how he and Spindle were sliding it along the top of one of the metal rails, each holding an end in their mouths and running, one squirrel on either side of the rail. Apparently this was Spindle's idea – he was good at finding easier ways to do things.

They rested under the bridge and told how they had got Chip away from the Temple Tree. It could only be a matter of time before there was a posse after them, but it was getting dark and there was a hint of snow in the air. The bridge would offer some shelter. Rather than press on and perhaps get caught in the open, they decided to spend the night there and move off in the morning. They all climbed to a ledge out of reach of any possible prowling foxes or dogs, and huddled together, shivering in the draught which blew through the archway.

*

Crag and Ivy had returned to the Temple Tree clearing later than usual. He was pleased with the success of that day's search. Dozens of Greys were following him, each carrying or dragging some metallic object. The hollows of the tree were nearly full, and this surely would convince the Sun that he, Crag, was a truly worthy squirrel. The grey female, Ivy, was proving to be an unexpected ally, urging the tired Greys on with reminders of the horrors of the Sunless Pit.

He could see there was some kind of commotion at the foot of the Temple Tree. Rusty was rolling about on the grass chattering incoherently, surrounded by guards who were trying to understand what she was saying. He shouldered them aside and Rusty fell silent.

"What's going on?" he asked roughly, addressing himself to her as she lay on the ground.

She did not reply, just rolled her eyes wildly.

One of the Greys said, "Temple Master, she has been raving since after High Sun. We did not know what to do."

Crag looked around. "Where is my son?" he asked.

"In the Temple Tree . . ." the Grey replied, his voice faltering as he realised the significance of the question. "That is, unless . . ." He stopped.

"Fetch him down, then," ordered Crag, icily.

The Chief Guard went slowly up one trunk, then the other, searching and calling at each opening, before returning to Crag on the ground, his tail low. He did not need to speak.

Crag scowled at him, looked to where the setting sun was disappearing behind a bank of wintry clouds, and decided that there was enough time for them to go to the Blue Pool.

With their overwhelming numbers, they could and would destroy the Blasphemers for ever. He ordered all the Greys to follow Ivy and himself and they left, ignoring the now motionless body of Rusty at the foot of the Temple Tree.

No sooner were they out of sight than she shook herself, brushed the dust and moss from her fur and scampered from the clearing, following the scent of her son and the two other Reds.

However, before long, being unfamiliar with the business of tracking, she lost the trail and wandered away southwards, hoping to pick it up again later.

Crag, without Marguerite's knowledge of numbers, was unable to estimate how many Greys were following him. The ground was covered in them, all chattering excitedly. More were in the treetops overhead, following him to destroy the Blasphemers and put an end to their sinful ways for ever. He, Crag the Temple Master, was going to do this – a worthy squirrel indeed!

Ivy followed behind, whispering in the ear of any laggards.

They reached the Blue Pool Demesne as the first snowflakes fell from the darkening sky, to find only deserted dreys. Crag ordered a search of the area, then, gnashing his teeth with rage, he turned and led his shivering grey followers back to the Temple Tree.

Chapter 26

Juniper was the first of the huddled squirrels to wake on the ledge under the bridge. He looked down and saw where the snow had blown in and partly covered the lines below him. Through the arch he could see that the ground was blanketed with snow to the depth of two standing squirrels, with the wind stirring it into drifts. Even high on the ledge he could hear the rustle of the wind-hardened grains as they blew along the surface, but there was another sound that he did not know, and it was coming from the lines themselves. They were whining like an animal in pain and the sound was getting louder, now accompanied by metallic groans. He leaned down from the ledge and peered outside. An enormous creature was coming along the lines towards him and was going to enter their hiding place – it must be seeking *them*. In panic he shouted, "Every squirrel, get outside. Run for your lives. Follow me!"

Juniper leapt down from the ledge and ran out into the snow, followed by a gaggle of half-asleep squirrels, stumbling and rolling as they scrambled from the shelter of the bridge into the cold white world. The "monster" had entered the shelter and now followed them out, roaring loudly.

Juniper jumped from the track and dived into a snow-drift, burrowing like a mole in his terror. The others, their hearts beating madly, tunnelled down behind him as the monster, ignoring them, rumbled on towards the little station of Corfe Castle village to engorge its breakfast of human travellers.

Deep in the snowdrift the squirrels lay, panting from their exertion, packed closely together, until, when they realised that the "monster" had gone, they relaxed and wriggled into more comfortable positions.

"What was that?" a youngster asked, but no squirrel could give a satisfactory answer.

The chamber enlarged itself as they jostled about and soon they were in a snow-cave, where each could crouch easily, snug against one another and surprisingly warm; it was certainly better than the draughty bridge-arch. They felt secure and safe deep in the drift and one by one dozed off and slept in the snow-cavern throughout all of that day and the following night, knowing that the snow had concealed their scent-trail.

Only one incident disturbed the calm. Tansy was snugging against the skinny body of Chip when Tamarisk tried to wriggle in between them.

"What do you want?" she hissed, keeping her voice low so as not to disturb the other squirrels.

"Just to be near you," Tamarisk replied, his mouth close to her ear; then he added, "I don't like the way you favour that squimp." Even as he said this he knew that it was a foolish thing to say, but it was too late. He felt her body stiffen and sensed the rejection.

"He's just left his mother to the mercy of the Temple

Master, and we know what *he's* like. If you weren't such a squaker, you would be out there helping her escape!" She elbowed him away and closed her eyes.

Tamarisk crawled up the tunnel and out into the cold whiteness. So that was what she thought of him, was it? He'd show her.

Several times the squirrels in the snow-cave heard the lines whine and groan as the "monster" passed, but as before, it did not attempt to leave its track and seek them out.

On the third morning a westerly wind blew in from the Atlantic, warm from the distant Gulf Stream, and the chamber in which the hungry squirrels huddled started to drip and collapse. Alder led them out into the open and after a little stretching and stamping around they set off again along the lines, the youngsters whimpering for food and being comforted by the older squirrels. Chip was constantly looking over his shoulder as though expecting to see his mother, but the others were more concerned with ensuring that there was not a posse of Greys on their tails. It was comforting to know that their scent would have dissipated into the snow and neither Crag nor the Greys would know in which direction they had gone.

The metal lines were clear of snow and the "monster" had pushed aside any drifts on to the side of the track, so the squirrels easily followed the rails as they curved round towards the ruined Man-drey they could see on the great mound ahead of them. Twice the party left the track and hid when they heard and felt the lines whining and vibrating, but on both occasions the "monster" passed without concerning itself with them.

The second time Rowan sat up and watched it. "It's not a "monster," he told the others. "It's just a lot of the box-things that humans travel about in, all joined together. I could see humans inside it."

After High-Sun they left the lines, went down an embankment, crossed a roadway and stared up at the piles of rocks towering against the sky above them.

"This is the castle," said Dandelion. "I didn't realise it was as big as this."

"Humans must have put all these stones on top of one another," Marguerite said, "though Sun knows why!"

Her youngsters were close to her side. "I'm so hungry," Young Oak told her.

"So am I," whimpered little Burdock. "We haven't eaten for days."

"We must find shelter first, then we will look for food," she told them.

Juniper said, "Where there are humans, I can find food. I used to be tagged the Scavenger once. Did you know that? If anyone can find human food, I can." He was almost proud, then realised that the Scavenger was a lowly tag, one to be ashamed of. How Life changed one's standards when the cones were down!

They all climbed the steep grass-covered mound to the ancient castle walls, dragging the Woodstock up with them, and then explored the rock faces, searching in every nook and cranny, looking for a safe and sheltered hiding place. It was Chip, more at home on the rock than the other squirrels, who found the cave, high up on an outer wall, half hidden by a mass of ivy stems and leaves. It was on the south side, so was protected from cold winds and not too distant from the humans' village, where they hoped to find food in the morning.

For many years jackdaws had used this cave as a nest site, so inside there was a mass of old sticks and sheep's wool that they could use for bedding, even if it did smell musty and unpleasant. It was dark by the time the Woodstock had been carried up the tangled stems to safety in the cave. Twice it had fallen and they had had to climb down to recover it, using the joint efforts of all the mature squirrels. Even so, none of them had noticed that Tamarisk the Forthright had not been with them all day.

Crag's temper had not improved as he led the horde of Greys back to the Temple Tree through the falling snow, and his black mood deepened when he found that Rusty had evidently taken the opportunity to desert him. She had always been unreliable, he thought savagely, much too prone to sentimentality and far too soft towards that youngster. Both of them were unworthy squirrels; he was better off without them! The Greys were harder workers and now he had Ivy on his side the metal collection was growing steadily. The Sun had evidently sent her to help him get the Greys to stock the Temple.

He crouched, shivering, in the cold chamber that was his lonely sleeping place, thoughts tumbling through his brain. If the Sun had sent the Greys to help him, it had probably also arranged for those two unworthy squirrels to be removed. He called down for Ivy.

"When did Rusty last collect metal?" he asked.

"Moons ago," she replied.

Crag cursed. All that time she had lived with him in the

sacred place, eating the bounty that the Sun had provided – and contributing nothing. Nothing! His teeth chattered with anger and cold. She didn't deserve to live.

Throughout the two days when the snow prevented any Sun-worthy work being done, Crag crouched in his chamber, listening to the movements of the Greys in the hollows below him, but taking no food, even when Ivy offered some.

After the warm wind caused the drifts around the Temple Tree to melt away, Crag came out on to an upper branch and called to the Greys to assemble on the ground below him. As those in the tree poured from every hole to join those already on the ground, he looked down, exulting in the sense of power. The clearing seemed to be alive with squirrels, all waiting on his word. He signalled to Ivy and she called for silence. The chattering stopped abruptly.

There was a small cloud between him and the sun, casting a shadow on the wood, though it was bright enough on the distant hills, and on the trees not too far away. Crag waited for it to pass – he wanted to be seen clearly by all below him – but the cloud seemed in no hurry and the Greys below started to get restless and whisper amongst themselves.

Seeing this, Crag spoke, his voice higher pitched than usual. He coughed and started again, "Fellow squirrels, although we are of different colours, we have worked together to the glory of the Sun by collecting sacred metal and filling this wonderful Temple Tree to prove that I – we – are truly worthy squirrels and will therefore avoid the terrors of the Sunless Pit. This Temple Tree is now almost complete, but" – he paused – "we have been hampered in our efforts by an unworthy female whose name I cannot even bring myself to say. One who has lived off the Sun's bounty, yet hardly ever carried even the smallest offering to this glorious Temple.

"In the name of the Sun and the power I have earned as Temple Master, I declare this female to be a Squarry!"

Crag waited for some strong reaction, but the Greys looked at one another in puzzlement and then up at him, as though waiting for an explanation.

Sitka called up, "Temple Master, this word is strange to us. As you know, our instructions from the Oval Drey are to adapt to, and adopt, your local customs, but we don't know the meaning of 'Squarry'."

"Ignorant fools," Crag said under his breath, then called down, "A Squarry is one who has sinned so dreadfully that it is our right – no, our duty – to see that they go to the Sunless Pit at the earliest chance. A Squarry must be hunted down and killed. This duty takes precedence over all others. Find the Squarry and kill her! No squirrel is to return until they can report her death."

His high-pitched voice reached all the Greys below and was also heard by Tamarisk the Forthright, hiding in the branches of the pine tree across the clearing. He crouched there wondering what to do next. Evidently Rusty was not at the Temple Tree and now the hordes of Greys were going to seek her as a "Squarry".

The word was unknown to him too; it must be a part of the cult these Portland squirrels had brought with them. It was certainly alien to his teachings. One of the Kernels of Truth said:

Squirrels have the right
To explain their own actions,
Fully – in silence.

There was no evidence, from what he had overheard, that Rusty would be given this right of explanation, in silence or otherwise. It seemed that she was to be hunted down and killed without a chance to explain her reasons. Suddenly his mission had taken on a new dimension: not only did he have to rescue Chip's mother to prove himself to Tansy, but he was now the defender of the ancient culture of the Reds.

Ivy was issuing orders as the Greys spread out in all directions to search for the Squarry. Tamarisk stayed put. They were unlikely to look in the tree nearest to the Temple, for they would expect Rusty to be some distance away by now.

The hubbub died down as the last of the Greys left the clearing, and Crag went back into the Temple Tree. Tamarisk contemplated crossing the clearing and tackling the Temple Master. He was younger and could probably win a fight, but this would be contrary to the very Kernel he was acting to defend. He would leave Crag to the Sun. In the meantime he had to find Rusty before the Greys did. Remembering Marguerite's absolute confidence that help would come when most needed, he recited the Kernel,

Have faith in the Sun
His ways are mysterious.
Faith can fell fir trees,

then looked around for some sign that might indicate the way to go. The little cloud that had hidden the sun from Crag had now expanded to fill the sky from horizon to horizon, though a small patch of Sunlight glowed on the side of Screech Hill away across the Great Heath.

Tamarisk felt drawn to the distant brightness, and set off through the treetops in that direction, pausing only long enough to eat some pine seeds, holding the cone in his paws and tearing away the resinous flakes protecting them. He would travel faster if he was not hungry.

Chapter 27

It was Chip who first noticed that Tamarisk was not with them in the cave behind the ivy on the castle wall. The squirrels were preparing to send a foraging party to the human village and Chip was steeling himself for the usual deprecating comments and unkind remarks that Tamarisk whispered to him whenever Tansywistful was not at his side. He looked around the cave in the faint light that filtered in through the leaves and the stems that partly covered the entrance. His antagonist was certainly not there. Perhaps he had gone out before the others? But then, as Chip thought back to when he had last been subjected to Tamarisk's taunts, he realised that he had not seen him since the last night in the snow-cavern. He spoke to Tansy, trying to sound casual. 'Have you seen Tamarisk?'

Tansy looked about, then called loudly, "Has anyone seen Tamarisk the Forthright?"

No squirrel could recall seeing him since the night in the snow, but there were pressing things to be done. The youngsters were whimpering with hunger, and food of some kind must be found. Tamarisk was a grown squirrel, with no family responsibilities; he must be left to his own devices, though some of them felt disappointed that he should have deserted them. However, as the Kernel taught them:

Each squirrel is Free
To choose its own route through Life –
Guided by Kernels.

Tamarisk had evidently chosen his own route, away from Tansy, who must seem unobtainable to him.

Rowan was once more left in charge of the youngsters, the Woodstock at his paw in case of any kind of attack, whilst all the other grown squirrels went to scavenge in the village.

Tamarisk was heading for Screech Hill, where the barn owls hunted, staying behind the searching Greys, whose coverage of the ground grew ever more sparse as the ring of squirrels spreading out from the Temple Tree got larger and larger. Eventually he was able to slip between the searchers unnoticed and, once ahead of them, hurried in the direction of the hill which rose to dominate the countryside, acting as a beacon for him.

Alone, he could travel fast. He was near the base of the hill before the winter dusk drove him to find shelter in a rotten tree, using the abandoned nest-hole of a woodpecker for shelter.

In the morning, encouraged by the dawn Sunshine lighting up the summit, he set off in that direction, strangely confident of finding Rusty somewhere near there.

And so it was. In the highest tree near the hill-top he

found her, trying to get warm in the weak rays of the sun. He went up to her and cuddled her chill form, warming her with his own body, which was glowing from the exertion of his climbing and running through the treetops. When she had thawed a little and her shivering had stopped, Tamarisk said, "I've come to take you to Chip", and was surprised when she said, "I shouldn't have run away. I think it's my duty to go back to Crag. I fear the Sunless Pit. Chip will be safe with your friends." The last word sounded awkward, as though she had never spoken it before.

"Crag has declared you to be something he calls a Squarry," he told her. "All the Greys are out to kill you."

Rusty shrank back in horror. "Me, a Squarry? He wouldn't do that to me!"

"He has," said Tamarisk. "You can't go back."

"I must. Perhaps if I go back, Crag will forgive me and cancel the Edict. Oh dear Sun, me a Squarry. I must go back, it's my only chance."

Tamarisk considered his options. He could abandon Rusty and find the others at the castle. She would then either live or die alone, or be killed by the searching Greys. Or he could try to escort her back through the ring of searchers in the hope that Crag would forgive her, or he could try again to persuade her to come with him to join the exiles and be reunited with her son.

All his efforts were in vain. He explained that the Sunless Pit was only an expression of somewhere awful and did not really exist, but soon he realised that her fear was deep-seated and terrible.

Rusty told him about the Sin-day and the awful night

and day that had followed it. She insisted on returning to Crag.

Tamarisk accompanied her, unable to face Tansy's scorn if she learned that he was too much of a squaker to see Chip's mother safely back to the Temple Tree, if that was her wish.

Together they passed unnoticed through a gap in the ring of Greys, now in groups, searching every patch of woodland and scrub, and through the deserted Demesne of the Blue Pool towards the Temple Tree. A storm was brewing and the silence was oppressive and unearthly. Thunder rumbled in the distance and Rusty looked around apprehensively.

The foraging party to the village had been successful. Most of the Man-dreys had had platforms on the grass areas behind them, laden with food which birds were eating. Jackdaws from the castle took first choice, landing and flying away with large pieces of bread. Then the starlings bustled and jostled each other over what was left. Blue tits and other small birds fed from containers of nut kernels and pecked at the flesh of some kind of huge nut, one half of which hung down from a branch near an opening in the side of one of the Man-dreys.

The squirrels moved in and drove the birds away, having no qualms about taking the food, which humans had clearly put out for other creatures' sustenance. Even if it was not wholly intended for them, they had hungry youngsters waiting up in the castle, and in such circumstances almost anything is "acceptable behaviour".

With hungry youngsters
Actions can be permitted
Otherwise taboo.

The party fed themselves, then returned to the castle cave, each squirrel carrying in its mouth the largest piece of food that it could.

Spindle and Wood Anemone worked harder than the rest, carrying the most awkward pieces and laying these down to assist others before returning for their own loads. Their actions did not seem unusual to the other squirrels, who had often witnessed such unselfish behaviour from the two ex-zervantz. The two, though, were carrying an additional burden that felt like a stone, heavy in their gut; they thought that they were the ones who, through their indiscretion in revealing the whereabouts of the food reserves, had been responsible for the Reds having to leave the pool. Neither could speak of their shame.

Late in the afternoon Chip suggested that he climb to the highest of the stone towers to look out and report. He was secretly rather looking forward to climbing rock again, anticipating the thrill of seeking each tiny hold in the apparently smooth surface and using these to climb up to a place where no other squirrel would dare go.

Alder, hearing the plan, insisted that Chip was not to go alone and Rowan volunteered to go with him if Chip would teach him to climb on rock.

He proved an apt pupil. Utterly fearless, he soon mastered the fundamental concept of three paws holding whilst the other was moved to a new hold, and together the pair climbed the great column of stone that is all that remains of the Queen's Tower of Corfe Castle.

They could hear the distant rumble of thunder that had disturbed Rusty away across the Great Heath. Rowan cautioned his young friend that if a storm came near, they would have to descend swiftly to avoid the danger of a lightning strike in so high a place.

Chip pointed out that the clouds were massing over the Blue Pool area and they would have sufficient time to get down safely if the storm did come in their direction. They searched the vast landscape spread out below them as far as they could see for any sign of grey squirrels, but saw none and were just about to descend when lightning slashed out of the distant cloud to strike somewhere in the wood near the Blue Pool. It struck again and yet again, unaccompanied by the usual rain and, as they watched, a spiral of smoke rose out of the trees where they had seen the flashes strike.

They climbed down in the gathering dusk, neither saying a word to the other yet each sure that the Temple Master would trouble them no more.

Tamarisk and Rusty had reached the Temple Tree as the storm clouds gathered and thunder rumbled over their heads, but Tamarisk had restrained Rusty's desire to go straight to Crag and ask forgiveness. He persuaded her to climb with him up the signalling tree across the glade first.

Rusty had clung to the branch and called, "Temple Master Crag, it is I, Rusty. I have come back to repent for my sins. I fear the Sunless Pit."

Crag's head appeared at the opening near the top of the trunk and he looked about.

Rusty called again, "It is I, Rusty, come to repent." She shook the pine needless to show him where she was and he climbed higher into the dead upper branches of the oak in order to see her better.

"You are a *Squarry*," he replied brusquely. "A Squarry *cannot* repent. You will die – and that will be an example to all squirrels. It will show that the Sun's will must be done. It is the Sunless Pit for you. When the Grey Ones catch you, you will die. Get out of my sight. I cannot bear to look on such an unworthy squirrel."

A shaft of light from the setting Sun shone almost horizontally from under the storm cloud, lighting up the red-brown fur of the Temple Master as he gesticulated wildly.

It was then that the first of the three flashes of lightning struck the tree.

Tamarisk and Rusty, nearly blinded by the intense light, edged backwards along the branch, dropped to the ground and scampered away towards the Blue Pool, followed by the scent of burning wood as the old tree flared orange and red behind them in the dusk. Tamarisk was sure that he could smell seared flesh and singed hair, but said nothing of this to Rusty.

They slept together in Tamarisk's drey near the pool, warm in the mossy lining, as the storm finally broke and rain cascaded down, rattling on the dead leaves. In the dripping dawn they returned to view the Temple Tree, watchful for any Greys. They saw none, but the Temple Tree itself had burned away, leaving nothing but a towering mass of fused metal that could, in the poor light, be mistaken for the form of a gigantic squirrel. They hurried away, the smell of damp wood-ash and scorched metal following them along the track.

Chapter 28

The cave in the ivy, high on the southern wall of the castle, was proving to be a comfortable communal hiding place for the squirrels from the Blue Pool. Each day a foraging party would raid the village bird-tables and return carrying sufficient food for the youngsters and whichever squirrels had been left on guard.

On the first day in the cave Tansy was her usual restless self, asking Marguerite how soon it would be before they could move on, with the Woodstock, towards Ourland. Marguerite pointed out that they needed to feed up first; many of the squirrels were thin and not fit for further winter journeying.

There had been no sign of Greys, and, although Tansy was missing Tamarisk more than she would admit, she was busy with instructing her Chipling in the ways of Mainland squirrels.

Marguerite fulfilled her role as Tagger and teacher, ensuring that all the young ones knew the ancient Kernels of Truth.

Ignorant squirrels
Not knowing all their Kernels
Will act foolishly.

Spindle and Wood Anemone were, unbeknown to each other, watching for a chance to speak to Marguerite. They respected and loved her dearly, but dreaded that a confession would result in a down-tag. Spindle the Helpful imagined being retagged the Indiscreet or perhaps even the Traitor! He could not bear the thought of that disgrace and once again not being able to hold his tail high.

Wood Anemone's imagination did not run to tags, but she feared the scorn of her friend Marguerite and the other squirrels. Yet she could not bear the weight of their secret. On one foraging expedition she spoke to Marguerite when the two were apart from the others.

"Marguerite ma'am," she started, as though she were still a zervant addressing a Royal, then started again as Marguerite shook her head. "Marguerite-Friend," she said, the words like ash in her mouth, "uz muzd tell yew something."

Marguerite heard the tale in silence. This was a stupid thing for them to have done and fully deserved a downtag, and yet . . . If she, Marguerite, had been conditioned by a lifetime as an obedient zervant, would she not have reacted in the same way? Was there any benefit in imposing down-tags on her friends? No – friendship must be left out of this decision. A True Tagger must be impartial.

Would a down-tag act as a warning and an example to others? The circumstances were unlikely to occur again. Did Spindle and Wood Anemone deserve punishment? Not really. The act in question was virtually automatic. One in authority asks; a zervant reports. Marguerite said the Understanding Kernel:

If you could know all
Then you could understand all
Then you'd forgive all.

"You are forgiven, Wood Anemone-Friend. Tell Spindle, and we will never speak or think of this again."

One afternoon, about a week after they had arrived at the castle, the squirrels were sitting in the ivy enjoying the spring sunshine, the snow now a fading memory. The ivy was good to sit in. The curves of the twigs made comfortable couches, the only drawback being the pungent smell, but by now the squirrels had learned to ignore this and often sat there while they built up their strength for the next stage of the journey.

With plentiful food and warmer weather, Marguerite felt that they should now prepare to move on in the direction that Dandelion had indicated would lead them to the Agglestone. She spoke to Alder and he agreed, so she went to tell Tansy, sure that she would be delighted with the news. She found her at the back of the cave, crouched in a corner shivering.

"Tansy-Friend, what's the matter?"

Marguerite was beside her, holding the slim body and feeling the heat of a fever radiating from the young squirrel.

"Dandelion, come quickly," she called over her shoulder, and together the older females settled the younger one in a nest of old sheep's wool and covered her over with more.

"I'll stay with her," said Marguerite. "If she's not better by morning, we'll look for some herbs, but it'll be hard to find anything until they start growing again in the spring."

Dandelion had promised a story that day and they had decided to continue with this despite Tansy's fever. As the youngsters gathered round, Meadowsweet, whose turn it was to be on watch and guard duty, called out, "Squirrels coming."

Rowan scrambled up beside her and looked in the direction she was pointing. Far below, at the foot of the castle mound, a pair of red squirrels were moving forward slowly through the tussocky grass, frequently looking behind them as they did so.

Although the travellers were obviously exhausted, there was something about the way the leading one moved which identified him to Rowan as Tamarisk. The other he did not recognise at first, but as they got nearer, he could see it was Rusty, Chip's mother. Both of them looked tired and travel-worn.

Rowan, Chip and some others went down to greet them and help them up to the cave.

"There are Greys following, not far behind," said Tamarisk. "Rusty is a 'Squarry'."

Only Chip understood the meaning and implication of this and he ran across to his mother and licked her face and paws. She hugged him to her, with no sense of sinning, and told him what had befallen his father.

When she had finished, he said, "I saw the lightning strike, Rusty-Ma. I think I knew then what had happened."

The others had gathered around Tamarisk, who was eagerly chewing on a crust of bread brought up that morning from a bird-table.

"Where's Tansy?" he asked.

Marguerite told him that she had a fever and was sleeping at the back of the cave.

Tamarisk looked concerned, but snatched another bite of the crust. "There are Greys following our trail. They are likely to be here before nightfall. I am sorry we've led them to you, but there was nowhere else for me to take Rusty. We hoped to find you somewhere here. Can I see Tansy?"

Marguerite and Alder posted extra lookouts and the Woodstock was positioned so that it would cover the entrance to the cave.

"We should be safe," Marguerite assured them all. "No squirrel will get past the power-waves and into the cave." She tested the weapon by scratching a Z on the soft wood after the permanent numbers 1 2 3 4 5 6 7 10 and her X which were already cut deeply into the wood. The invisible power that spiralled from the end of the Woodstock was sensed by their whiskers, though not seen by eyes or heard by ears. The ivy leaves around the entrance curled up into tight little tubes.

"They won't pass that force!" Marguerite said.

Rusty and the youngsters, who had never seen the Woodstock in action before, were impressed and comforted.

"Squirrels coming," Rowan called from his lookout point. "Greys, lots of them."

The senior squirrels peered down from the cave entrance and watched a posse of Greys following the scent-trail of Tamarisk and Rusty.

"Do we give them a chance to talk, or do we just use the Woodstock when they reach the cave?" Alder asked, seeking guidance from Marguerite.

"From what Tamarisk and Rusty have told us, they are not going to listen to reason," she replied, "but we'll try to talk to them."

They waited until the Greys had reached the base of the wall and stopped to regain their breath. Their leader was the broken-toothed female they called Ivy.

"What do you want?" Marguerite called down to them.

"We have come to kill the Squarry, Russty. "Iss she with you, Blassphemer?"

"Yes – and here she stays. The Temple Master is dead, so you can abandon your mission." She was bluffing – Rusty had told her that a Squarry Edict could never be lifted – but perhaps the Greys did not know that.

"You lie, Blassphemer," Ivy called back. "Send the Squarry out to uss and you can leave here unharmed."

"I should warn you that we have a weapon whose power would amaze you," Marguerite called down. As she said this, she wondered if these Greys knew how to create the Stone force which their compatriots had used the previous year. If they did, they could trap the Reds in the cave and starve them out.

The Greys ignored what she had said. "We give you until sunrisse to hand over the Squarry," Ivy called up, "then we come for her, and any squirrelss, old or young, maless or femaless, who ressisst will be killed and sent to the Sunlesss Pit."

She did not believe what the Reds had said about Crag being killed. Anyway, it no longer mattered to her. He had served her purpose. No Grey dared disobey her orders. This power was a wonderful thing. She, a mere female, ignored and overlooked for so long, now had only to mention the Sunless Pit and the others scurried to fulfill her commands. If only I had learned how to use the Stone power that the old regime had used to subdue these Reds, she thought, I would have the whole of Squirreldom in my power.

She directed her party to take up positions on ledges on the wall, out of reach of dogs or cats from the village, and they crouched there to wait until sunrise.

In the cave the Reds discussed the chances of their creeping out in the darkness, unobserved.

"We can't, with Tansy ill, and even if we succeeded, they would follow our scent and catch up with us in a less secure place," Marguerite pointed out. "Trust in the Sun," she added, "and the Woodstock.

Your prayers alone
Won't do. The Sun will help those
Who will help themselves."

A youngster's voice from the back of the cave said, "Can I help myself to a nut? I'm hungry."

The laughter that followed broke the tension and the squirrels settled down to a watchful and uneasy night.

Juniper reported the first movement of Greys in the dim light of dawn and moved back into the cave behind the Woodstock, rehearsing the numbers to release its power. A 1 after the X did nothing, whereas a Z created a modest force and a 3 was definitely a "whisker twister" at that short range. Numbers higher than that would probably kill. He would start with a ʒ. There was no point in killing if he could disable the attackers effectively with a lower number.

There was a disturbance in the ivy leaves and he could see a round-eared head silhouetted against the light. He immediately scratched a ʒ and felt the force fill the cave entrance. He heard the leaves rustle as a heavy body fell out of control to the ground outside.

A second face appeared and he scratched a ʒ again. More rustling and then another thump as a second body fell.

No more faces appeared, and after a while Juniper and Rowan peered cautiously out. There was a cluster of Greys below them, gathered around two others who were pawing at their faces.

Juniper knew from his own experiences that the Woodstock power could curl a squirrel's whiskers into tight spirals and the only way to stop the spinning in one's head was for the curled whiskers to be bitten off. This, though, left the whiskerless animal unable to climb or balance properly. On his own initiative, he sighted the Woodstock at the cluster of Greys and scratched a ʒ into the wood.

The cluster broke apart, squirrels tumbling and rolling down the bank, all pawing their faces. The Reds came forward, gathering at the cave entrance to watch the helpless Greys and to congratulate Juniper.

Marguerite drew Alder to the back of the cave to discuss their next action. Tansy appeared to be sleeping at last. They spoke quietly.

"If it wasn't for Tansy, I'd suggest that we left now while

the Greys are in disarray, but she's in no fit state to travel and we can't leave her here."

"Yes you can," said a shaky voice from behind her. "You must get the Woodstock to Ourland. I can follow when I'm well again. I've travelled on my own before, remember."

"We're not leaving here without you. You need our help to get better. A few more days won't make much difference. We know that this is a good defensive position and it's quite likely that the pine marten is dead anyway by now. Try and sleep, Tansy-Friend."

It was more than a few days before Tansy was well enough to move. Her fever raged on, sometimes easing a little, only to return with even more vehemence. They knew that they were being watched by Greys from the hillside opposite, but small parties went out each day searching for different herbs to ease Tansy's fever. Foraging parties visited the village bird-tables daily for food, though for her own safety Rusty always stayed in the cave, sharing the duty of nursing Tansy with Tamarisk and Chip.

The Hawthorn Leaf Moon and the Catkin Moon had both gone before the fever died, leaving Tansy clearheaded but as weak as a new-born dreyling.

The effect of the Woodstock had come as a shock to Ivy and the Greys. Not a single Grey from Purbeck had survived the previous year when the Woodstock had been used in an attempt to destroy their Power Square, so it was completely unknown to them.

When Juniper had used it on the group below the cave, the Greys had all retreated to lower ground. Some had their whiskers curled into tight spirals, others had whiskers that were loosely curled and those who had been close under the castle wall, including Ivy and Hickory, were unaffected. Sitka's whiskers waved like ripples in sand.

"Hickory, Sitka, join me," Ivy commanded. Hickory came at once, though Sitka seemed slower to respond and wandered about before coming to Hickory's side.

"It seemss that the killing of the Squarry iss not going to be ass eassy ass we exspected. The Redss have some weapon that we know nothing of."

Her mind was working fast. She knew that this was a critical time. Her authority rested primarily on her relationship with Crag, who the Reds had told her was dead, and on her false claim to have been sinless, reinforced with her constant reminders of the horrors of the Sunless Pit. Was this enough to prevent them from turning on her, as so often happened to a leader defeated in a battle?

She looked at the other Greys. The majority were in no state to challenge anything. A retreat and regroup was called for now.

"Hickory. The mosst important tassk iss to be yourss. Select two other squirrelss who have not been affected by the Redss' sinful sorcery and watch their every actionss. I will lead the otherss back to the Temple Tree to recover and then we will find a way to kill the Squarry ass we have been directed. If there iss any sign of the enemy leaving, send a messenger to me and follow at a disstansse. Do you undersstand?"

Hickory looked at the other Greys, most of whom were pitifully trying to straighten their whiskers with their claws. He thought briefly of just hopping off to start a new life away from all this peculiar business of metal collecting,

Squarry hunting and that coldness, that terrible lonely coldness. Then he remembered the Sin-day. He was not going to risk falling and blindly spinning down, down, down, for ever.

"Yes," he said. "I understand."

Chapter 29

If there was a frustrated pine marten anywhere in the world, it was Blood. After days and days of searching for the squirrels he now knew where they were.

He had found their scent often, but each time, just as he was expecting to surprise them resting, the scent-trail led him down on to the beach and disappeared. He could not believe that the whole party had taken to swimming away each day.

There was a spring warmth in the air when he saw them again. He was prowling behind the island castle near where the last of the peafowl were living when he spotted movement in the treetops. He froze and watched a column of squirrels pass overhead, then climbed a tree and followed silently to discover where they were hiding.

Old Oak always took the last position in the line as they made their daily evasive movements, looping in from the coast as the tide covered their scent-trail on the beach, to find a temporary hiding place, only to move on again at low tide. Twice each day Just Poplar insisted that they did this, and they were all exhausted now, but none more so than Oak. His joints were stiff and he often thought of asking

Clover or one of the ex-princesses for some herbs to help, but he knew that it was age, not illness, that was slowing him up. He reflected on how well the two, Voxglove and Cowzlip, frail as a result of generations of Royal inbreeding, had learned Clover's Caring secrets, leaving her free to develop her role as a Tagger.

Oak was also impressed with the way Clover had grown into that role. Coping with the distress and disruption of their lives caused by the pine marten and her experience of caring for the sick ones had given her a deep insight into squirrel behaviour. All agreed that the tags she allocated were true and fair, and that her advice to the Leader and to the Council was always sound and impartial.

Old Oak was resting, gathering strength to run and catch up with the others, when he saw a movement in a tree in the direction they had come – only a glimpse of brown fur and a flash of white on the chest. At first he thought that some squirrel had fallen behind, unseen by him. Then, with horror, he realised that it was the pine marten – coming his way!

Learning of danger
Leap, scramble, climb, hop or run,
Warn all the others.

He paused. That was the Kernel for this situation. He must warn the others, but he knew that he didn't have a leap or a scramble left in him, let alone a climb, hop or a run. There was only one other action worthy of an ex-Leader. His life was nearly at an end anyway. He rustled the branches to attract the marten's attention and dropped to the ground.

One of the wardens, walking under the trees, looked up

as he heard the sound of the leaves moving, but was not prepared for what happened then, as a squirrel dropped from the branches above and lay still at his feet. He crouched to look at it; its tiny chest was palpitating with fear and its eyes were fixed on something above his head. He looked up again but could see nothing unusual. When he looked down, the squirrel had gone.

Oak caught up with the others where Just Poplar had called a halt once he had found that Oak was not with them.

"The pine marten was following us," the old squirrel said breathlessly. "But a man with the sign of Acorn, the first squirrel, on his chest frightened him away. You should have seen the look on that marten's face – he was terrified of that man!"

Just Poplar, remembering the time before the "Acorn" men came, said, "If he *is* afraid of humans, perhaps we should live amongst them. They have never harmed us."

They all thought about this for a moment.

Clover agreed. "That's right, they never bothered us at the Blue Pool. Yes, let's go and live among the humans. I'm tired of all this hiding."

The weary squirrels climbed over the wall of Brownsea Castle and slept in the shelter of the great sequoia tree there, secure in the belief that the marten would not come so close to where the humans were living and working.

When the late winter finally turned to spring, the Ourlanders were there, marvelling at the activity of the busy humans below, who were clearing the rampant growth of decades of neglect, trying to get everything ready for the scheduled reopening of the island to the public in May.

The squirrels had seen the pine marten in the distance several times and on each occasion they had moved nearer to wherever the humans were active that day, and had watched the marten turn away in fear.

Although by now mating should have been under way and dreys prepared for a new batch of dreylings, no squirrel had felt the urge, even when the sun had warmed them. Their lives were still unsettled, and the constant presence of the marten, though at a distance, was disturbing. How soon would it be before he overcame his fear of Man and attacked?

Ivy reached the Temple Tree clearing at the head of a posse of tired and demoralised Greys. They had taken three days for a journey that could be done in a single day by a fit squirrel, but few were fit. At the end of the first day those who were unaffected bit off the curled whiskers of the others. This did at least stop them wandering around in circles but none of the whiskerless ones could climb and they progressed on the ground, terrified of being found by foxes or dogs.

The Reds had said that the Temple Master was dead. We'll soon know if that is true, Ivy thought, as they came through the last of the trees surrounding the clearing. They stopped and stared.

Where there had once been a great oak tree there was now a gigantic squirrel – made of metal, each piece joined to the next. The squirrel-shaped mass stood on its hind legs, towering above them, its tail high and an accusing look in the eyes formed by two metal discs. Ivy remembered those discs; Crag had been very proud of those. They had been in the centres of larger round things beneath one of those human travelling-boxes and they had shone in the sunshine when Crag and a gang of Greys had levered them off with sticks. Crag had insisted that they were taken to the highest point in the Temple. Now they were partly blackened by fire, but, like Crag's own eyes, they glowered down balefully on the tiny animals below.

"What has happened to Crag?" Sitka asked, his voice wavering.

"Can't you see?" snapped Ivy. "The Sun hass made a metal squirrel out of him to remind uss all that we musst never forget to follow hiss exsample and obey hiss appointed successor – Ivy the Sinlesss. Now search for another hollow tree which even the whisskerlesss oness can get into for safety. Trusst your leader. Hate the Squarry. Go now and look for hollow treess."

Chapter 30

"That must be the Agglestone," Rowan called back over his shoulder.

The other squirrels peered through the heather and bracken in the direction he was pointing. Half a mile away a great rock was propped up at a steep angle, resting on other rocks; it was several times a human's height, but there were no humans near at this time of day. The sun was low in the sky and darkness would not be far away.

With Tansy at last fit to travel and all the other Reds eager and anxious to be out of the confines of the cave, Alder and Marguerite had sent out a scouting party to check on the grey watchers. They knew where the three had their position, in a scrub oak on the bank opposite the castle mound, and the scouts circled round until they could see that all three Greys were there. They reported back.

"We leave before dawn tomorrow," Alder had announced. "We must be clear of the castle mound before it gets light enough for the watchers to see us go. We will head south, though we believe the Agglestone to be to the east. If we are followed or seen, this will help to fool the Greys.

Later we will take the true course. I think Marguerite has a Kernel about that."

The unexpected,
Obscure action, confuses
Squirrels' enemies.

They had left unseen in the pre-dawn darkness and headed south.

Earlier on the day they first sighted the Agglestone they had passed through a strange countryside. Long strips of short grass ended in patches where the grass was even shorter. The squirrels had marvelled at the pigeons' eggs which humans were unsuccessfully trying to smash with sticks; the eggs eventually rolled into holes in the ground, when the humans would lift them out and try smashing them again. It was all most perplexing!

Now Alder looked around for a tree in which to spend the night, where they would be safe from fox-danger, but there were none near enough for them to reach before it got dark. The air was still warm from a day of spring sunshine and the rock ahead looked as though it could offer protection, if not much in the way of shelter.

"Make for the rock," he said. "We'll spend the night there. Don't hurry; forage as you go."

The moon was rising out of the sea when they reached the Agglestone and, as the great silver globe lit the heathland, the tired band of travellers looked up at the dark mass towering above them. Alder and Rowan prowled around the base to find a way up.

There were a number of places where an agile and

unburdened squirrel could climb, but they had the Woodstock with them.

"What about this?" asked Juniper, his paw on the twisted spiral of wood.

"I think we can safely leave it down here," Alder replied. "There's been no sign of Greys since we left the castle mound. Hide it in that holly bush."

He indicated a dense mass of holly a squirrel-leap or more from the base of the rock. The shrubby mass had grown only to the height of three squirrels, most of each spring's new growth having been nibbled off by deer before the prickles had had time to harden.

With Rowan's help, Juniper pushed the Woodstock in under the bush, trying to avoid the spiky leaves, whilst the other squirrels were climbing up the rock with Marguerite in the rear. She had stopped on a ledge and was examining some shapes cut in the face of the stone, presumably by humans. Stark in the moonlight, they were like her numbers but different. One – F – she had seen on the ship that had passed them on the sea the previous year, but the others were new to her. There was a K, a W and many others. What could these be for? she wondered. She pointed them out to Juniper and Rowan, but they were more concerned about climbing up and finding a safe place for the night.

Together they scaled the steep side of the great rock, which stood alone like an island in a sea of heather, and found the others settling down in hollows near the top where tiny plants with fleshy leaves grew in the crevices. The moonlight made the scenery eerie and unreal.

"I'll take First Watch," said Juniper the Steadfast, and

the others did not demur, even if First Watch was favourite as it meant an uninterrupted sleep thereafter. Juniper was, after all, the oldest of the party and, with the hardships of the journey, his age was beginning to show, although he did his best to hide it.

Alder always took Last Watch, the one before dawn, as this too meant that his sleep would normally be uninterrupted. They had all agreed that it was important that the Leader was well rested so that his decisions would not be affected by tiredness. Other watches were allocated by rota.

Rusty settled down beside Chip. She had been practising warm actions on their journey, both towards her son and to the other squirrels. It certainly felt good and made her glow inside. She was learning new Kernels every day. Her favourite was:

You will be much loved,
No matter what else you lack,
If you are just kind.

Rusty savoured the Kernel and tried reversing the lines:

If you are just kind,
No matter what else you lack,
You will be much loved.

It meant the same thing that way, only somehow stronger, rather like seeing a reflection in still water, where the upside-down image was often brighter than the real one. How she loved being with her new friends!

*

A tawny owl was hooting to signal a successful night's hunting as Marguerite shook Alder awake for Last Watch.

She had watched the stars fading from the sky as dawn neared. A Man-light far out over the sea to the east glowed steadily then went out twice in quick succession, then glowed again. It had kept repeating this obscure signal and she had wondered what it was for. Then she turned her mind to the strange Man-carvings on the rock below. What did they mean? Why had men spent time cutting them? What was the significance of the shapes being mostly in twos or threes? She decided to take another look in daylight before she left the rock in the morning.

She had been away from the Blue Pool for so long, the sense of loss at leaving it was diminishing and she was almost enjoying the challenges of the journey, though a deep-seated fear for her parents on Ourland gnawed at her insides. She tried to tell herself that she was doing all she could to get there and that Tansy's illness had unavoidably held them up, but her mind started to go down the "but what if" path. She shook herself. She had taken the action that she had honestly believed to be the best at the time. If events subsequently proved it to be wrong, so be it.

Looking behind you
There is never any mist,
The view is superb.

She smiled as she thought of Tansy, now comfortably asleep between Tamarisk and Chip, who in turn was snugged against his mother, Rusty. Tansy and Tamarisk were together most of the time, Tamarisk much less tense since his rescue of Rusty. He would be due for an up-tag soon, she must put her mind to choosing a suitable one. And Rusty might like her name changed to that of some flower, following the tradition of the Mainlanders.

Chip's dependence on Tansy had lessened during her fever and he spent most of his time with his mother, who was eager to learn all the customs and the traditions of the Mainland squirrel culture. She knew many of the important Kernels. Although initially unsure of herself, which Marguerite put down to a lifetime of dominance by the Temple Master, she was learning that females could and should play active roles in all squirrel affairs. It would soon be time to allocate her a tag as well as a new name.

When Alder had taken over watch, Marguerite snuggled down next to Juniper and closed her eyes, but the strange shapes paraded across her eyelids – FK WS. She tried counting the corners to see if they were numbers. F had three but there was already a number for that. K had three as well and so did W. S had none, like her figure O. Soon she was dozing, warmed by the body heat of her life-mate.

Alder sat on the highest point of the rock, watching the sky lighten in the east. He had come to enjoy seeing the sun rise on these early watches: first the almost imperceptible fading of the blackness, then a hint of grey light as the birds began their dawn chorus. Then any eastern clouds would catch a trace of pink on their lower edges and gradually, so gradually, the light would get stronger and the birdsong louder, until the edge of the sun peeped over the horizon and day had really begun.

This was the time when he had to wake the others, and he was about to do so when, out of the corner of his eye, he saw a movement. He turned but could see nothing out of the ordinary. There were little grey wisps of vapour rising from the ground – it must have been one of those he had seen. Then, just as he was about to turn away, he saw another movement in the same place – a stealthy movement. *Something* was out there, coloured grey, and creeping towards them along the sandy path they had used on the previous evening. It seemed that the Greys had found their scent-trail and followed it! Still unsure, and not wanting to cause unnecessary alarm, he went down and quietly woke Juniper and Rowan.

Alder whispered to them, telling of what he thought he had seen, and the three of them went up to the highest part of the rock. No movement could be seen in the heath scrub and Alder was about to apologise for a false alarm when Rowan saw the heather-tops shaking. Soon it became apparent that there was movement all around the rock.

Alder decided the others should be woken and Juniper quickly went to do this, whispering their fears to each group of squirrels. Rusty's teeth started to chatter and she had to clamp her jaws together. Chip crouched close beside her.

"It's going to be all right, Rusty-Ma," he whispered. "These squirrels will protect us if it *is* the Greys."

The Agglestone would form a good defensive site, Alder was thinking, should it prove necessary. The rock behind them was steep, overhanging in places, and the Woodstock could be used to cover the sloping front face. He looked round for it, then, with horror, remembered that it was on the ground, hidden in the holly bush.

"Dear Sun," he said, quietly, "*don't* let it be Greys."

Then he heard Ivy's voice. His prayer had come too late.

Chapter 31

Hickory had been bored sitting day after day watching the castle mound for signs of the Reds leaving. Each day he saw parties going down to the humans' village and returning later and, although unable to count very well, he knew that it was not all of them, and he never caught a glimpse of Rusty the Squarry.

In idle moments he thought of just moving on westwards and leaving that crazy Ivy behind. He regularly sent his fellow watchers back to report, and from them he knew that Crag was dead or, as the more simple of them believed, had been changed into a giant metal squirrel. Ivy was behind all that, he was sure. But if he did go westwards, he would be on his own and might never meet other squirrels for the rest of his life. Then there was the business of the Sunless Pit . . . No, he would stay for a time and see what happened.

Jackdaws were carrying sticks into the cave. He looked again. It was true. They would not be doing that if the Reds were still there. He felt sick. They must all have slipped away in the night.

Hickory shook his fellow watchers and cursed them for

not being alert and the three set off down the hillside, crossed the stream by a fallen tree and went cautiously up to the foot of the wall below the cave. Had the jackdaws not been flying in and out, he would have suspected a trap and feared the whisker-curling power that the Reds had. But, convinced that they had gone, he climbed up to find the cave empty of squirrels.

He sent one of the watchers to tell Ivy that the Reds had at last moved on, and with the other Grey close behind him, followed a fading scent-trail southwards.

Ivy, at the head of a posse of Greys, had caught up with him four days later, following the marks, symbols and scents he had left to guide her. Now they were looking across the heath at a huge stone outlined against the dawn sky.

Earlier, Hickory had seen the Reds dragging the twisted stick along and had guessed that it was the source of the whisker-curling power they commanded. He had suggested that they stop at a distance from the rock and find out where this stick was.

"Go down and challenge them, sinful one," Ivy had instructed him. "Then we can tell if the power workss outsside a cave."

This is a different Ivy, Hickory thought. She's got much more confident of herself while I've been watching the cave. Now she's expecting me to sacrifice my whiskers for her!

"It is obvious that the power works only on sinful squirrels," he replied. "As you are free of sin, you can go safely and see if they have the power stick with them."

Ivy looked disconcerted for a moment, then, realising that her whole basis of authority had been openly challenged, replied, "Cowardly one, if you are afraid to show yoursself, then I musst do thiss tassk mysself."

She gave him a scornful look, signalled to the other Greys to hold their positions and hopped down the path, her heart beating fast, knowing that she had gambled everything on this one act. She stopped and studied the sloping stone face in the growing light. She could see many red squirrels, but could not see the twisted stick that Hickory had described to her. Neither could she see any place on the rock where it might be hidden.

Risking all, Ivy stood to her full height and called up.

"Send down Russty, the Squarry, and we will leave you in peasse, Blassphemerss though you be."

Alder said nothing, but signalled to the senior squirrels to take up defensive positions, the males at the lower edge of the sloping face of the rock and the females where they could repel any Greys who might try to clamber up the rock to their rear. The yearlings, toughened now by the hazards of the journey, were to form a reserve in the middle and be ready to fill any gaps in the defence.

"Send down Russty, the Squarry," Ivy commanded again.

"She stays with us," Alder replied.

"Squirrels in trouble,
Always stand by each other
None suffers alone."

"Then you will all die together," Ivy replied. "The Temple Masster hass taught uss that *nothing* musst stop uss fulfilling the Squarry Edict."

"The Temple Master is dead," Alder called down.

"That may be so," Ivy replied, "but hiss Edict standss. Now, send down the squarry!"

Alder felt a body press against his as he stood, looking over the edge of the rock, wondering what to do next. It was Rusty.

"I'll go down," she told him. "My life is not worth all of yours."

Rusty felt a paw on her shoulder and looked around. Marguerite had anticipated her intentions and had joined her where she crouched next to Alder. She told Rusty,

"Evil will triumph
If good squirrels don't resist –
Even do nothing."

"That's true," said Alder. "We stand or fall together. Now, both of you, back to your positions."

Marguerite went up to the highest point. From here she could see all around. By leaning out over the edge she could see Greys on the ground, studying the rock for ways to climb.

She counted them, then turned to look in the other direction and tried to count the squirrels there. These had now come out of the heather and were milling around on the bare sand where the vegetation had been worn away by the hard feet of human Visitors, as though they knew the Woodstock could not be used on them. Some more Greys could be hidden from her sight beneath the overhang of the stone's lower edge. The Reds were well outnumbered and they had left the Woodstock down in the holly bush. She blamed herself for not insisting that they had carried it up the night before; she had been too interested in those shapes cut in the rock. Those would not save them, but the Woodstock might have.

Looking behind you
There is . . .

Too late for that now.

They did have the advantage of height, though. If it came to a fight, it could go either way. Trust in the Sun!

"Death to the Squarry. Death and the Sunlesss Pit for all thosse who protect her," called Ivy.

"Death and the Sunless Pit," chanted the other Greys, and the attack commenced.

The Reds held strong positions at the edges of the rock and were able to bite and scratch at grey paws and faces as the attackers tried to come over the rock-edge, but with their extra numbers and greater size and strength, the Greys were soon driving the Reds back up the slope. Juniper, at the lowest point, though slashing and biting in all directions, was unable to hold back the pressure from below.

On the upper edge the females were having more success. Every time a grey climber reached the top of the rock two red females would bite its paws and the Grey would drop backwards, yowling with pain and twisting in the air to land upright; it would then have to retire and lick the wounds on its crippled forepaws, unable to take any further active part in the fight. Another would take its place, however, and there was never a moment's respite for the defenders.

Marguerite was praying as she fought, facing the Sun.

Please help us, great Sun
To defend our beliefs – so
Evil may not win.

Across the heath near Wych Farm a geologist pressed the button that exploded one of his test charges buried in the ground, the echoes from the rock formation far below confirming the existence, and indicating the extent, of a vast reservoir of oil. Oil formed by vegetation which had grown in the Sunshine of a primitive earth, long before squirrels or indeed any other mammal had evolved.

He checked his instruments and moved across to connect the batteries to the second charge.

As Marguerite said the last line of the Kernel, the great ironstone rock, glowing red in the light of the early sunshine, trembled under their feet, and the squirrels, red and grey, clung on apprehensively.

"The Sun is with us," called Marguerite, and the Greys retreated down the rock, dropped to the ground and clustered together at the base.

"The Sun iss with *uss*," Ivy shouted, the words hissing past her broken tooth. "It iss shaking the rock to disslodge the Blassphemerss. Follow me, the Sun iss with USS!"

The Greys rallied and their attack recommenced.

The Reds were now hesitant in defence, but Marguerite called loudly from the top of the rock, "The Sun is with US. It shook the rock to discourage the attackers!"

Beneath their feet the great slab of stone trembled again, and each side, believing that the sign was favourable to them, fought more resolutely.

As the sun rose higher, the greater numbers and strength of the Greys were telling and they were pressing the Reds back towards the top of the rock. Juniper disappeared under a ball of grey bodies which rolled backwards and fell to the ground, limbs flailing in all directions.

The red defence faltered, and the Greys pressed home their advantage. The whole of the lower half of the sloping rock was a seething mass of grey pressing upwards against a thin line of Reds. Alder turned to signal for the reserve of yearlings to engage the enemy, only to find that they were already in action, fighting in pairs. Somehow they had broken off flakes of rock and one of each pair was leaning over the edge hammering at the Greys whilst the other held on to its back feet.

In the thickest part of the action Tamarisk was fighting side by side with Rowan.

"I wish we had the Woodstock up here," he said, between slashes at a grey male who was trying to outflank him. "That'd knock a few off the rock!"

Rowan leapt back to avoid a savage bite from another Grey, and replied, "Could we get it? It's worth a try, we're losing here. Nothing venture . . ."

"Follow me," called Tamarisk, and, with Rowan at his side, ran between the startled females, judged the distance, realising as he did so that he had never made such a jump before, and leapt from the rock to land in the holly bush.

As Rowan jumped a grey head appeared over the edge of the rock in front of him and a grey paw reached up and caught his leg as he flew over. The Red and the Grey fell, fighting, to the ground below.

Tamarisk, in the holly, wriggled his way down through

the spiky leaves which pricked his skin painfully. A needle-sharp spine pierced his left eye and, though he felt the stab of pain, he fumbled around amongst the stems in the shadow of the dark green leaves until he felt the smooth twisted shape of the Woodstock.

The Greys on that side of the rock, intent on trying to avoid the teeth and claws of the defending females, ignored the "deserter" who had appeared to abandon his companions and was probably fleeing for his life somewhere behind them. They could hunt him down later.

Tamarisk, half blinded by the blood pouring from his left eye, pushed the Woodstock some way out of the bush and directed it at the Greys at the back of the rock. He was about to scratch a ʒ when he saw a flash of red fur amongst the mass of grey. He held back, wondering what to do.

Rowan's head came up out of the mêlée. He called to Tamarisk, "Use the Woodstock – now!" and the head went down again.

Tamarisk brushed away the blood from his face, aimed it into the writhing mass and scratched a ʒ just as the great rock shook for the third time. Then he directed the power of the Woodstock on to those Greys clinging to the sunlit side. They felt agonising pains around their mouths and nostrils and, with their heads spinning and their claws no longer able to hold on to the crevices, they fell backwards, to land in moaning heaps on the ground. Here they lay, pawing at their faces and trying to straighten the tight curls now seemingly burned into their previously straight whiskers.

Engrossed in their own distress, the Greys ignored Tamarisk as he attemped to drag the Woodstock round to the other side of the great stone.

A grinning Rowan was suddenly beside him, helping. "I turned my back, got my head down and hid my whiskers," he said breathlessly, in answer to Tamarisk's unspoken query.

"I'm glad you're here. My eyesight's funny – I can't judge distance."

Rowan sighted the Woodstock and scratched a bold ȝ.

The grey reserve on the ground, watching the fight above and ready to clamber up to join in if called on, didn't notice the two Reds with the peculiar stick until too late. The spiralling force struck them and they fell back, pawing at their faces. The Reds above, now assisted by the females, who no longer had to defend the rear, pushed down the rock, driving more Greys into the range of the Woodstock.

Soon only a few, including Hickory, were still able to fight. There was no sign of Ivy. Alder called a halt and the two sides each withdrew a squirrel length and paused, facing each other, panting for breath, but with the Reds' tails conspicuously high.

Marguerite came forward and, having got a nod of assent from Alder and unable to see Ivy, addressed Hickory.

"The Temple Master is dead. The Temple itself has been destroyed by the Lightning Force and now, with the help of the Sun, your party is defeated and your compatriots will have to suffer a whiskerless life for at least a moon. Will you accept that this squirrel, Rusty, is no longer to be what the Temple Master called a Squarry?"

Hickory lowered his tail as a sign of submission, but said nothing.

"Where is the female you call Ivy?" Marguerite asked.

Hickory shrugged his shoulders, but another Grey called

up, "She is here, Red One."

Ivy's body was dragged out from under the rock, Juniper's teeth through her throat.

Rowan went across to Juniper and put his paw on the bloodstained chest of the old squirrel, then did the same to Ivy.

"They are both Sun-gone," he announced.

"Deal with your injured," Marguerite said to Hickory. "We will talk more later."

She climbed to the top of the rock to be alone.

Chapter 32

Marguerite looked down on the Greys at the base of the rock. The few without injuries or curled whiskers were helping the others. She felt sorry for them and in a way responsible. They had come to her asking to be taught native ways and because she had sent them away, they had fallen under the influence of the fanatical Temple Master. Because of this, her life-mate, Juniper the Steadfast, was Sun-gone along with several Greys, and many more squirrels were hurt. The Reds had been forced to leave the Blue Pool and were now in the middle of a heath with no trees near to give Juniper a proper burial *and* they still had to get to Ourland and tackle the pine marten.

Turning her head, she could see Ourland over the water beyond the heath. If only she could see if the pine marten was still there, but it was much too far away.

To her right was the sweep of a sandy beach and over the sea beyond that she could just see white cliffs. Further to her right were the rock columns where the dolphins had come to her rescue the year before. She thought of them, Malin and Lundy, and wondered if they were, even now, out in that vast expanse of sea.

She looked down at the Greys again. They had come to the Blue Pool to learn native customs. She knew from the intensity of her Sun-scene that her destiny had to be on Ourland, but she asked herself briefly if she should not go back with the Greys and teach them the Kernels of Truth and how to live at peace with nature and one's surroundings. It also seemed important that the cold creed taught them by the Portlanders should be permanently replaced with one of Love under a friendly Sun.

She felt drawn to the idea of staying. She wanted time to work out the meanings of the humans' carvings on the rock. Her life-mate was Sun-gone, her youngsters were strong and healthy and could get along without her. But . . . a Tagger's first duty was to her community . . . and she did so want to know what had happened on Ourland since she had left. She sensed that Old Burdock had gone to a worthy rest, but hoped that Oak and Fern, her parents, had not been taken by the pine marten.

She couldn't stay; she was the only one who really understood the power of the Woodstock, and that would be needed there to destroy the marten. No – *she* couldn't stay!

Rowan, whose injuries from the fight were relatively light, was having similar thoughts about the Greys. He was discussing them with Meadowsweet, his beloved life-mate.

"Some squirrels ought to stay and teach these Greys all the Kernels," he was saying. "If they are going to be the new Guardians, some of us must teach them the proper way to do it. Would you stay with me if I offer?"

"Rowan, my love, where you go, I go. Where you stay, I stay. Young Bluebell too."

"If we are going to keep our kind alive on the Mainland,

we will need more than one family to stay. Should I ask the ex-zervantz?"

Spindle and Wood Anemone, although realising that they might never see Ourland again, readily agreed to stay on with their two youngsters, if the Council approved. Wood Anemone especially was glad that she would not have to make a sea-journey again.

The matter was discussed and settled at a Council Meeting held on the rock after High Sun. Hickory and two others of the "whiskered" Greys had been invited to attend as part of their retraining. They appeared to welcome the offer of help from Rowan.

The body of Juniper was buried near the holly bush, as the next best thing to a tree. The Reds, with the Greys behind them, gathered round to say the Farewell Kernel to a valiant fighter and a squirrel who had learned his wisdom through severe hardship.

Sun, take this squirrel
Into the peace of your earth
To nourish a tree.

The bodies of the dead Greys were buried on the side of the holly bush and, with Hickory's permission, the Farewell Kernel was said for them as well.

Then, whilst the sun was still quite high, Rowan and his party led the low-tailed Greys away across the heath in the direction of the Blue Pool, planning to reach the safety of a tree before darkness overtook them. They moved slowly, the injured Greys hobbling as best they could and the few whiskered ones among them guiding the others.

An emotional farewell had taken place in the unspoken

knowledge that it was unlikely that they would ever meet again, and the remaining Reds climbed to the top of the Agglestone to flick the "farewell" signals with their tails until the departing squirrels were out of sight over the ridge.

Marguerite half expected Tansy to ask if they could move on, with the Woodstock, at once, but Tansy was more concerned with Tamarisk. She was at his side all the time helping him move about. The sight in his left eye had faded and was now lost completely. It was obvious to Alder and Marguerite that at least the rest of that day and a night of recuperation would be needed before they would be able to travel.

While they rested, Marguerite turned her attention to the Man-carvings on the rock, but there seemed to be no pattern to them.

The intensity of her concentration kept thoughts of the loss of Juniper and the departure of her brother and his family from her mind. She was no nearer understanding the meaning of the shapes cut in the rock when she realised that it was too dark to see them. She had not eaten, but was too weary to care, so she climbed up and joined the others high on the rock.

"I think we can do without keeping a watch tonight," said Alder, hardly able to stop his tail-stump from dragging, as he crawled painfully to the shallow scoop in the rock where most of the others were already asleep.

Marguerite agreed. No squirrel could have stayed awake in any case. They were all too exhausted and would have to accept whatever risks the night might bring.

*

The moon was high in the sky and the stars sparkling and twinkling above her when Marguerite woke feeling refreshed. She looked for the pattern of the Great Squirrel and followed the line of its paws to find the "Star that is always in the North". That was the direction in which Ourland lay, she was thinking, and she climbed to the top of the rock to see if she could see it in the moonlight.

Her attention was drawn to the Man-light across the sea. It glowed, then died, glowed briefly again, died again, then glowed steadily. Then the signal was repeated. Was it trying to tell her something? She stared out across the sea, concentrating hard.

Her whiskers were tingling in a way she had only experienced once before, when she had found that she could communicate with dolphins without actually speaking. She moved her head from side to side until the tingles were equal. Into her mind came gentle voices, like the soughing of the wind in distant pines, and she focused on these until the voices became clear.

"Can you hear us? Is that the small creature we were able to help last year? We sense that you have been part of a great triumph. Truth and fairness have beaten evil and bigotry. If it is you, we join you in hope."

Marguerite concentrated her thoughts and stared into the night towards the flashing light.

"Yes, it is I. Greetings to you both."

"We are three now. We, Malin and Lundy, have been Sun-blessed and have a youngster. We call him Finisterre. Your voice is faint. Are you far inland?"

"I am on a great rock in the middle of a heath, a day or so's travel from the sea."

"You are leaving the Mainland." It was a statement, not a question.

"Yes, I am needed on the island in the great pool."

"Your destiny is there."

This too was a statement, and Marguerite recalled Lundy telling her that dolphins could sometimes "look forward". She had been right in deciding not to return to the Blue Pool.

"The day after tomorrow we will come into the sandy bay. If you need help, speak to us again then. Farewell."

The voices faded and an owl called tremulously from across the heath. Marguerite felt a curious mixture of loneliness and hope.

Chapter 33

The squirrels had got to the sea.

Marguerite had told Alder of her contact with the dolphins and he had decided to have a meeting on the rock to discuss the next course of action. The most direct route to Ourland was north across the heath, but then they would have to find some way to cross the water themselves. If, however, they headed eastwards, they would reach the sea in the direction from which Marguerite had heard the dolphins' voices, and they had promised help. But in that direction were many Man-dreys, with the possibility of meeting dogs. Finally it was decided to head north of east until they reached what appeared, at that distance, to be a tree-covered knoll with a deserted part of the coast beyond it. They hoped that the dolphins would find them there.

It had been hard work for the depleted party, several of whom were injured, to drag the Woodstock across the heath and it had taken them all of that day.

They had slept in pine trees on the knoll on which there was a large Man-drey, but with no scent of the dreaded dogs, and from the pines they watched humans coming and going in their travelling-boxes, their actions as incomprehensible as always. For spring, the foraging there had been good, and even better when the humans had noticed the squirrels and had put out a variety of foods for them behind the Man-drey.

In the early morning Marguerite had asked Alder to summon a special Council Meeting for a tagging ceremony. This had been held in the highest of the pinetops, a warm breeze blowing in from the sea and rustling the needles gently.

"It is sad when a Tagger has to allocate down-tags," Marguerite had said, her face stern, then, as the squirrels had looked at one another in dismay, she had smiled and added, "but a joy when up-tags are to be given."

There had been an audible murmur of relief.

"Firstly, I propose to up-tag Tamarisk the Forthright. After his brave action turned the tide in the Battle of the Rock, he has earned the tag Great Leap. He will now be known as Tamarisk Great Leap. All in favour?"

There had been nods of approval and tail-flicking all around. Tamarisk's one good eye had glowed with pride.

"Tansy the Wistful," Marguerite had continued, "has shown great courage and fortitude in coming to us to seek assistance for our comrades on Ourland. My proposal for her is Tansy Stout Heart."

There had been more approving nods and tail-flicks.

"Finally, Rusty and Chipling, our friends from Portland, who until now have had no tags. For Rusty I propose Rusty the Kind, and for Chipling, as he wants us all to call him, the tag Who Seeks Love."

Chipling had looked a bit disappointed, but had to agree that, with Tansy now preoccupied with Tamarisk, it was a true tag and he had vowed to himself that he would earn a better one soon.

The plentiful food and the pleasure of the tagging ceremony had put the squirrels in high spirits as they crossed the roadway when it was clear of traffic and struggled through the sand dunes, dragging the Woodstock with them.

They paused at the top of the last dune, the marram grass high above their heads, and listened to it rustling as the salt-laden breeze, blowing in from the sea, bent the tops of the grass landwards.

Apart from some seagulls pecking amongst the wisps of seaweed at the high-tide mark, the beach was deserted in the morning sunshine. The squirrels crouched in the shelter of a clump of the coarse grass and waited. Several of them, tired from the struggle over the dunes, slept fitfully, sand blowing into their ears and nostrils.

As the sun got higher, some humans walked up the beach from the south and took off their coverings, replacing them with smaller pieces before sitting on the sand. A few, mostly young ones, ran into the water, shrieked and ran back up the beach.

Near High Sun, when the heat of spring warmed the squirrels comfortably, they watched several of the humans venture into the water and swim around aimlessly before coming out and sitting or lying on the sand again.

There were no swimmers when Marguerite felt her whiskers tingle with the dolphin vibration. She stood up and looked out to sea. Two large dolphins and one small one curved up out of the water and slid back down into it with hardly a splash.

One of the humans had also seen the dolphins and, calling to the others, ran down to the water's edge, pointing and gesticulating. The humans stood up and looked the way the man was pointing. The dolphins appeared to ignore them.

All the squirrels were alert now, standing and staring out to sea. The three black backs curved through the waves.

"Are you there?" a voice in Marguerite's head asked, and she knew it was Malin "speaking".

"Yes, except for my life-mate, Juniper, who nourishes a holly bush, and some who have chosen to remain, we are here."

"Stay in the sand-grasses until it is dark, then we will bring a boat to take you to your island in the Great Harbour."

"Do dolphins have boats?" Marguerite asked.

"Not of our own," came back the reply. "We'll use a boat of the humans."

"Will they let you?"

"They won't know it is us. If they miss it, they'll think it is other humans; they are always taking one another's things. We will bite through the rope and when we have finished with it, we will push it ashore at high tide where they can find it. Without hands like theirs we can't re-tie, but we will leave the boat where it will be safe."

"Is it 'right' to do that?" asked Marguerite, remembering the Kernel:

If not in your care,
You must ask the Guardian –
Before you use things.

"In principle, no. But humans no longer hear when we 'speak' to them. And considering what *they* are doing, we have no qualms about using a boat now and then," replied Malin, with an unexpected tinge of bitterness in his "voice". "The way they treat the Sea!"

"How is that?" asked Marguerite, thinking of the humans she could see, clustered at the water's edge.

"They pollute it, that's how," came back the reply.

As Marguerite watched, the three glistening bodies curved up out of the blue of the water again. She marvelled at how that simple action, which a minute before indicated peace and contentment, now expressed anger and resentment.

"This beach, the one they call Studland, is one of the few that are really clean now. But at many places along the coast they pour their dung into our Sea."

Malin continued, sadness replacing the anger in his voice, "Only a few days ago we swam up the Channel past the Man-dwellings in that place the humans call the English Riviera. They are very proud of that place and their dwellings are all along the coast and up the hillsides."

Lundy's thoughts washed over Malin's. "The squirrels are not concerned with this. They have problems of their own that we are here to help with."

Malin ignored her. It was obvious from the strength of his thoughts that this was a major concern of his.

"We took a short cut between Thatcher Rock and the

Mainland near there, and human dung was streaming out of the end of a tube on the seabed, tainting the water for miles."

"I thought humans buried their dung like cats do," said Marguerite, remembering the Flood story.

"They may have once, but now they just pour it into the Sea. I wonder how they would like it if thousands of dolphins sprayed *their* dung into the air over the land!"

Marguerite thought of the squirrel saying:

People puzzle us
With their strange actions – but then
They're only human.

A moment of appreciative thought carried across the waves, followed by, "I wish it was as simple as that, but there are disturbing metallic tastes in the Sea now, especially around the estuary of the Great River and up the coast to the north of it. It made young Finisterre quite sick when we took him up there. Sometimes it is hard to find clean water near the coast at all!"

Marguerite did not know how to reply, there was so much sadness and concern in the dolphin's thought-voice.

Then she heard Lundy again. "I am sorry to bother you with our problems. Malin gets washed away sometimes; pollution is a real peril to us and we feel so helpless, unable to do anything about it.

"We will leave now and come back when the moon sails the sky. We will have a boat for you then. Listen for us."

Out in the bay the three black shapes curved out of the water and vanished again below the surface. The humans waited for a while then drifted up the beach and settled down on their towels to enjoy the sun and the breeze on their bodies.

It was now uncomfortably hot on the dunes and, though shaded a little by the marram grass, the squirrels lay panting in the heat. They could hear the waves on the beach and the cries of seagulls and excited young humans at play, but were not disturbed.

As the sun dropped in the sky, the humans re-covered themselves, gathered up their things and wandered away along the shore. When they were out of sight, Dandelion, remembering her days on the beach at Worbarrow the year before, led the squirrels down to the shoreline and showed them which seaweeds were edible, and they raced the seagulls to any scraps of food left by the humans.

The sea had been going away from them, but started to return as darkness fell. The squirrels sitting in groups on the sand felt vulnerable, but completely confident that the dolphins would return, bringing with them a "boat", though the yearlings had no real idea what such a thing was.

Chip, at his mother's side, was watching Tansy washing and cleaning Tamarisk's blind eye with her tongue. Tansy Stout Heart was still kind to him, but her main concern was with Great Leap, though Tamarisk was more subdued than he had ever been, and gave more thought to his words before he spoke.

Rusty, after knowing for a lifetime that a Squarry Edict was "until death", could not really believe that she was free and safe amongst these wonderful, warm-hearted squirrels, and kept glancing towards the heath, fearing the return of the Greys to impose the Edict.

Alder was restless. He had never been in a "boat", and he was apprehensive. He had grown to trust Marguerite's judgement and had no qualms about the integrity of "her" dolphins. But he was about to commit his whole party to some new experience out of his control and at the end of it they would be landing on an island strange to him. Then they might have to tackle a pine marten, the ancestral enemy of all squirrels!

This whole venture was absurd, though he seemed to have no choice but to go along with it. He would have to trust in the Sun and not show his fear.

When the cones are down,
Even if you doubt yourself,
Hide all your concerns.

Dandelion wondered if she should tell a story to pass the time, and was about to call the youngsters together to hear one when the edge of a huge yellow moon rose above the horizon, casting weird shadows on the dunes and the beach. The squirrels, with the fear of attack by Greys behind them and the island with the pine marten still somewhere in the future, seemed strangely moved to be in the open, under this odd light. Before long some of the yearlings were scurrying up and down the beach, turning sharply in flurries of fine sand and leaping over pieces of flotsam.

Squirrelation took over, all caution thrown to the night wind, and the beach became alive with leaping, running and scampering squirrels of all ages, until Marguerite, who had briefly forgotten the loss of Juniper, called, "The dolphins are coming."

The excitement changed to anticipation as the outline of an unmanned rowboat appeared and was driven on to the sand by a push from one of the dolphins swimming behind it.

The squirrels clustered around the severed mooring rope hanging from the bow, nudging each other, until Marguerite, who had clearly taken charge, said, "Up the rope, one by one", and the squirrels climbed as swiftly as they could, and disappeared over the gunwale.

Marguerite gave one last look around the beach to see that no squirrel had been forgotten and followed the others up the rope.

Chapter 34

Flapping and splashing in the shallows, the dolphins turned the boat in the rising water and towed it out to where Finisterre, their calf, was waiting, poking his head above the waves as he swam back and forth anxiously watching for the return of his parents.

As they reached Finisterre, a current caught the boat and moved it southwards, parallel to the shore. The dolphins sensed Marguerite's concern that it was going in the wrong direction and Malin spoke.

"We use the currents. It would be possible to push the boat all the way to your island, but we can guide it from current to current and get there effortlessly and just as quickly. Trust us."

The three dolphins swam alongside. Marguerite wondered if they would leap, as she had seen them do from the beach. No sooner had the thought formed in her head than the three black bodies, gleaming in the moonlight, curved up and out of the water, to the astonishment and joy of the squirrels standing on the rowboat's seats. The presence of the dolphins seemed to have banished the squirrels' instinctive fear of water and all were enjoying themselves, giving little thought to the hazard to be faced when they reached the island.

The dolphins cavorted and leapt all around the boat as it drifted along, until finally, when they knew it would not frighten the squirrels, they leapt in unison right over the boat. Drops of salt water rained down from their tails on to the animals below, causing the youngsters to shriek with delight.

Then, as a current caught the boat and bore it inexorably towards the narrow mouth of Poole Harbour, Marguerite asked, "Won't the humans see us?"

"They are mostly asleep at this time," came the reply from Malin, "but they are usually so concerned with their own immediate affairs that they notice little else. Did they see you on the beach?"

"No," replied Marguerite, "but we kept ourselves hidden in the grasses on the sand and watched out for them. Why did some of the humans go into the water? They just swam about and came out again."

"It's an ancestral memory that prompts them to do that. Do you recall last year that we told you how dolphins once lived on the land and then went back to the sea again. Well, humans nearly did the same. It is in our History Training.

"Far, far back in time, when humans stopped being creatures of the trees, they lived on the ground in dry places for aeons and then, when these got too dry, they lived on the coasts of the country they now call Africa. They spent most of their time in the shallow water where they were more comfortable walking upright, and it was then that they lost most of their body hairs, keeping only enough on their heads for the Man-cubs to cling to when their parents swam. It was at that time that scent became unimportant to them and they had to learn to be clever with their voices so that they could communicate with each other whilst they were swimming."

Marguerite was trying to keep up with the mass of new images passing through her brain. It was tiring, but she was determined to learn all that she could from these wonderful and helpful creatures who had befriended her and her companions.

"Do humans remember that time?" she asked.

"I don't believe so; they don't teach Long History as we do. But when the sun starts to get warm each year, they follow old urges and make for the Sea. They still love to swim for the pleasure and the feeling of being in the water. I sometimes wonder what would have happened if they had carried on evolving that way until they became totally creatures of the Sea as we dolphins did. They still shed tears, you know!"

"What are tears?"

"Nature gave us sea mammals a special place in our eyes where we can get excess salt out of our systems. Humans still have these, but they only use them when they are distressed. They should use them all the time, knowing how they are treating our Sea!"

"Malin, leave that," said Lundy, severely.

"Humans are strange creatures," Marguerite agreed, "though harmless to squirrels as far as our memory goes. But we don't trust them fully; so much of what they do seems inexplicable. We have a squirrel saying:

If you could know all
Then you could understand all
Then you'd forgive all."

"For 'Innocents', you squirrels certainly think a lot!"

The other squirrels were unaware that any conversation was taking place, as Marguerite had learned that it was only necessary to think her questions, and did not have to speak them out loud. Most of the others were dozing on the floorboards by now, though Rusty and Chip were watching the Man-lights at the harbour entrance getting nearer, as the current bore the boat that way.

"What do you call an 'Innocent'?" Marguerite asked.

"We call all 'small-brained' creatures 'Innocents', as they just have to survive and breed and do not concern themselves with moral issues. I sometimes envy them."

Marguerite felt slightly offended at being called "small brained", but then realised that physically it must be true.

"We meant no offence," Malin assured her. "It can be a burden to be involved with greater issues than which fish you fancy eating today, or if your mating approach will be reciprocated.

"Most 'Large-brained' sea mammals carry this burden. Sometimes we try to communicate with the 'Great-brains', the whales. Their intelligence is *awesome*. You should hear them sing their philosophies!"

Malin was silent as Marguerite tried to understand the concept of "singing" and could only get a pattern of rising and falling voices in her head. She felt her "small-brain" limitations.

Lundy's voice flowed in. "We cannot understand why

humans kill the whales. Perhaps it is some kind of jealousy. The whales know things about the meaning of Life which even *we* can't get our minds around!"

"Perhaps they eat them," Marguerite ventured, remembering the unicorn in Dandelion's story of the Flood.

"Oh, no, it can't be that," replied Malin. "Humans are 'Large-brains' like us. They couldn't be *that* short-sighted and stupid."

The conversation ceased as the dolphins steered the boat into the centre of the channel between the points of land that formed the entrance to Poole Harbour. As the narrows passed behind them, Lundy said, "We will take you to the other end of the island. The humans have made a structure there which will help you all get out of the boat easily. Then we must hurry to get the boat back to its place before dawn."

The moon had set and grey light was creeping into the sky as the boat was pushed in against the pier at the western end of the island.

Marguerite sensed the dolphins' concern about returning the boat, and urged the sleepy squirrels to scramble out on to the pier. Her head was aching after a night of such intense concentration and she climbed out last, almost falling into the water as the dolphins, in their haste, started to push the boat away.

She remembered to thank them, urging her tired brain to project her thoughts: "Thank you, and farewell."

"Farewell, your Sun be with you," came back three simultaneous replies as the boat moved away out of sight around the point and past Woodstock Bay.

Marguerite recalled that that was where she had found the first Woodstock on the beach. Who had the New Woodstock? She looked around, then realised with horror that they had left it in the marram grass behind Studland Beach.

Chapter 35

Marguerite hurried along the pier after Alder, and drew him to one side.

"We have left the Woodstock in the dunes at Studland," she told him. "It's my fault. I was carried away by the dolphins and the boat and . . . I'm sorry, I should have remembered it."

"You've many things on your mind, Marguerite-Friend. *I* won't blame you for it. I should have thought of it myself, but I got caught up in the squirrelation. And then the boat came."

He rested his paw briefly on her shoulder. "We will have to get along without it. But first we must get everyone hidden in case that marten is about. Trust in the Sun."

They slept most of the day in some rhododendron bushes where they felt that any enemy approaching on the ground would betray itself by the rustling of leaves, and the dense foliage would keep them from being seen from the trees above. The breeze was from the south-east, so their scent would be blown out over the sea. Even so, they were restless and unhappy.

Tansy was eager to be off, to look for her parents, and

was torn between her concern for them and for Tamarisk, whose eye was still painful. She was also worried that there was no squirrel-scent at that end of the island at all. Were all the Ourland squirrels dead?

In the late afternoon and evening Alder allowed them to forage, a few at a time, and then insisted that they pass another night in the rhododendrons. Marguerite spent most of her foraging time unsuccessfuly searching for another Woodstock, feeling guilty that her forgetfulness had left them without its power when they needed it so much.

At dawn they moved off together above the old Man-track along the centre of the island, keeping to the trees and listening and watching out for any marten-danger. They saw rabbits and a sika doe with her fawn, and the heronry was raucous with the calls of the young birds, but there was no scent of squirrels or marten. At High Sun they rested in the great pines near the middle of the island where the exiles had first met the Royals nearly two years before.

Blood was angry and frustrated. There was food all about him: nestling birds, eggs for the taking, young rabbits just waiting to be eaten, peafowl at the snap of his jaws. He wanted squirrel, he needed squirrel, he deserved squirrel – but they were too close to the humans for him to dare to attack there. Thoughts of the time when he was caged flooded over him. He couldn't risk that again, even for squirrel.

There were only a few peahens left now, and the cock bird, Mogul. In the spring sunshine Blood watched them on the Man-track below where he lay on a branch high in a tree behind the church. The peacock was behaving differently. He usually dragged that stupid tail of his around behind him, trying to keep it out of the mud, but today he had somehow made it stand up behind him and he was strutting about so proudly, showing it off to the hens.

Not much to be *that* proud of, Blood thought, seeing it from behind. Then, as the male bird turned and the Sun caught the front of the tail-fan, he was dazzled and even Blood had to admit that it was special.

Arc after arc of gleaming iridescent eyes patterned the most beautiful long, bluey-green feathers and caught the Sunlight as the bird strutted back and forth in front of the admiring hens. The blue of his neck and the little bobbly crest flashed and glimmered, but Blood was no longer an admirer. In his frustration he was a despoiler.

He leapt down from the tree and, caring nothing that men might be near, ran openly across the grass towards the huge birds. The peacock's tail-fan collapsed in an instant and the birds scattered. Blood followed the peacock. Mogul ran faster and faster, then, realising that he was losing the race, launched himself heavily into the air with a screech of anger, and flew down the track to land on the branch of an oak, seemingly out of reach.

Blood followed on the ground, climbed the tree-trunk and ran out along the branch. The peacock, still breathless, shrieked, launched himself into the air again and headed for the Man-tree with the thin vines reaching out to the next "tree". He landed awkwardly on one of the power lines, trying hard to keep his balance as the wire swung to and fro.

Blood was not to be outdone. He dropped from the oak, ran to the foot of the Man-tree, wrinkled his nose at the scent of creosote, dug his claws into the barkless wood and climbed. Two thin leafless vines stretched out to the next Man-tree on either side, on one of which sat Mogul, watching the marten with his head on one side, ready to fly off again.

Blood knew that he would have to move fast. Reaching past a shiny white thing, he grasped the thin vine with a forepaw whilst holding on to the trunk with his feet. There was a flash inside his head brighter than the light on the peacock's neck, and he was falling, falling, falling through a pit where the sun never shone. Falling, falling, falling. Then a thud and – nothing.

Mogul screeched in triumph, lost his balance, fell backwards and fluttered to the ground.

By the time he had walked back to the group of staring hens he had recovered his composure. As they gathered around, he raised his tail as though nothing had happened. Blood was forgotten in the primeval mating display.

Later, a man with one of Acorn's badges on his jumper buried the pine marten's body in a place in the meadow where the peahens had scratched away the turf, and it was in the dry soil above Blood's grave that the peachicks played and dusted themselves through the long hot summer that followed.

Chapter 36

Oak and Just Poplar had been together in the sequoia tree when Blood had first chased the peacock. Oak's eyes were not strong now, so Just Poplar had described what was happening, his voice mounting in excitement.

When Blood fell, lifeless, from the power lines, Just Poplar was overcome with relief. At first he could not believe that their enemy was truly Sun-gone. It was not until he saw a human pick up the limp body and carry it away that he really allowed himself to believe what he had seen, and he ran off to tell the news to the other Ourlanders foraging in the castle grounds. Oak limped stiffly along behind him.

"The marten is Zun-gone, the marten is Zun-gone!" Just Poplar called and the other squirrels looked up, then gathered round to hear how it had all happened.

"Him wuz chazing the great bird who flew on to won of the vinez of the new Man-treez, and the marten climbed the trunk. The Zun zent a little lightning flazh to ztrike the marten and protect the great bird. Uz zaw the flazh, but there wuz no thunder. Let uz thank the zun."

The squirrels were unable to believe this. Could it all

have happened so quickly? They stood looking at the breathless Poplar, hope wrestling with disbelief.

"You're quite sure of all this?" Chestnut asked doubtfully.

Oak had reached them and confirmed Just Poplar's story.

"I saw the human pick up the body. They wouldn't do that with a live pine marten!"

Clover the Tagger moved forward, a Kernel forming in her head:

We thank you, oh Sun,
For freeing Ourland from the
Fear of the marten.

Then wild squirrelation took over. With the sudden removal of the one thing in the whole of Ourland that they feared, their relief exploded. Squirrels raced up and down the trees, leapt across pathways and capered wildly, to the delight of the humans who were streaming ashore from a fleet of boats for the official reopening of the island by the National Trust, and for the rededication of the church, on that sunny day in May.

The humans on the ground, and the squirrels in the trees, swept inland towards the little island church, whose tower, for so long the home of the scourge of Ourland, showed above the treetops.

Mogul, the peacock, strutted and displayed as if he knew that he alone was responsible for *all* the celebration.

It was a far more sombre party of squirrels who were progressing through the island treetops from the west.

Going slowly for the sake of the injured squirrels and the

one-eyed Tamarisk, Marguerite and Tansy were aware that, if the Ourlanders were safe, and had survived the attacks of the marten, there ought to be squirrel-scent in the trees. But they had reached the centre of the island without finding any.

They moved cautiously on eastwards.

The jubilant Ourland squirrels watched the humans as they entered the stone building until there was no room for any more. Other humans clustered outside in the sunshine. The males were wearing dark coverings and sweating in the heat, the sun hot on their bare heads, whilst the females were in bright coverings of many colours, and each had a different-shaped cover on her head.

The squirrels peered down in amazement. They had never seen such a gathering of humans, or seen them in such a happy mood.

Oak whispered to Just Poplar, "It looks as if the humans are celebrating a Sun-day."

It was then the singing started, never before heard by these Ourland squirrels. Waves of human voices, in unison, were rising and falling in rhythmic patterns like the sea on the beach, or the wind in the pinetops. Each squirrel sat and listened in rapture.

As suddenly as it had begun, the singing stopped and a single human voice was heard, the words meaningless to the squirrels.

Oak looked around. His fading sight had caught a movement in the trees to the west and for one awful moment he thought the marten was alive and stalking them. Then, realising that this could not be true, he pointed the movement out to Just Poplar, who peered in that direction.

"It's squirrels!" he called out, nearly falling from the branch. "I can see Marguerite and Tansy and Tamarisk and . . ."

His voice choked with emotion. Then the whole band of Ourland squirrels raced through the treetops to greet their friends.

Such hugging and whisker-brushing, such joy and sadness, so many stories to be exchanged and the death of the pine marten to be rejoiced over that, when the human singing began again behind them, they hardly heard it. Marguerite, sitting with her father, Oak, was hearing how her mother, Fern the Fussy, had died in the Bunker, when she felt herself moved by the rising and falling sounds and wondered if the singing of the great whales sounded like the singing of the humans in the church beyond the trees.

When the boats had taken most of the humans back to the Mainland, Marguerite, Tansy and Tamarisk explored the area around the church. They marvelled at how it had been cleaned up and how the overgrowth that they remembered had been cut away and burned.

Marguerite discovered that the humans had just planted a tree near the church. She examined its shape and the way the young branches stood out from the stem and even tasted the bark carefully, but could not indentify it.

If the humans are planting trees, perhaps they are beginning to use their "large brains" again, she thought, then raced across the grass to join the others who were returning to Beech Valley to celebrate their all being together again and to start rebuilding their dreys.

Chapter 37

In the summer that followed there were so many things for the squirrels to do. There were Guardianships to be allocated and established, and life-mates to be chosen by the yearlings. Soon the trees were alive with courting rituals and mating chases. Tails were high all over Ourland.

There was speculation as to whether Just Poplar would propose a life-mating between himself and Marguerite. It seemed to many to be a natural outcome, but she was withdrawn and preoccupied. Perhaps she was missing the comfort of Juniper's presence or was concerned about Rowan, Meadowsweet and the ex-zervantz with their huge task of educating the Second Wave of Greys on the Mainland.

Then at the Longest Day Celebrations Just Poplar surprised them all by announcing that Rusty the Kind, or Rush as she now preferred to be called, had consented to be his life-mate, and she joined him in the Council Leader's drey in the tree above the pond in Beech Valley. Chipling was delighted.

Tansy Stout Heart and Tamarisk Great Leap became

life-mates as expected, and took a Guardianship near the church. Tansy loved to watch the humans and listen to their singing whenever they celebrated a Sun-day, which seemed to be once every week. Her journey to the Mainland might not have been successful in bringing the Woodstock back, but it had resulted in her finding a truly appreciative life-mate and she knew that soon she would have a family of dreylings to tell her story to.

Chipling, though fully grown, attached himself to Marguerite and became her willing pupil. He did not appear to be interested in any of the yearling females now that Tansy was unobtainable.

Marguerite was pleased to have a listener. It was Clover, the established Tagger of Ourland, who taught Kernels, Traditions and Manners to the youngsters, and yet Marguerite was an elected Tagger as well. The squirrels of Alder's party were pressing for her to act as the official Tagger – at least for them.

Sensing that a dispute might develop which could spoil the new peace of Ourland, Marguerite and Clover, calling on the wisdom of an ancient Kernel, decided to get the squirrels to resolve it by Tail Pairing.

Big disagreements
Are only settled safely
By a Tail Pairing.

Marguerite, who knew from the traditions how a Tail Pairing worked, thought that she had an easier way to arrive at a result. Instead of matching a "yes" squirrel with a "no" squirrel and seeing which side those left over represented, she proposed a Tail Poll as she and Chip could both count above eight.

She was concerned to see how much the issue of who was to be Tagger divided the squirrels.

The two ex-princesses, now jointly tagged the Carers were vociferous in their support for their teacher, Clover. Voxglove, knowing that Alder would back Marguerite, put it around that he should not have a vote as he had no tail to signal his preference.

Clover and Marguerite joined forces to quash that suggestion. "It is the brain which votes; the tail is only used as a signal," Clover told Voxglove sternly. "Alder has other ways of making his intentions clear."

Chipling, being the only other squirrel besides Marguerite who knew numbers above eight, was very proud to be appointed to count the votes.

Excited squirrels gathered in the Council Tree on Poll-day. Just Poplar took charge. Fortunately there had been no conflict between him and Alder for the Leader's position; Alder was a recent incomer and had no desire to take on the responsibility. Mentally exhausted from the trauma of leading his party to safety through the early part of the year, he was glad to be able to live a quiet life on this lovely island with Dandelion.

"Squirrels who wish Clover to be Tagger, move to the south-side branches and raise your tails," Just Poplar directed. "Those who wish Marguerite to be Tagger, move to the north-side branches and do the same." Just Poplar moved to the south.

Chipling, very positively on the north side, started the count, mumbling the words to himself. Marguerite had already counted quietly to herself and knew that they were evenly divided. It was going to have to be settled by a drawing of twigs!

Chipling finished his count and a thought crossed his mind. He could ensure that Marguerite would be elected and no one but Marguerite would know. He glanced at her. She read his thoughts and shook her head.

He was about to declare "Equal Acorns" when old Oak slumped across the branch where Burdock had passed to the Sun a year before and, losing his grip, fell to the ground below.

The squirrels scrambled down to find that the fine old squirrel, Oak the Cautious, was truly Sun-gone. Later that day they buried him beneath the Council Tree near his friend Burdock.

Sun, take this squirrel
Into the peace of your earth
To nourish a tree.

The count was never declared. Marguerite, sad at losing her beloved father and recognising defeat without his vote, "climbed down" and wandered the island seeking a role for herself. Clover, seeing her thus, offered to share the Tagger's position.

"Thank you, Clover-Friend, but it wouldn't work. A True Tagger must accept total responsibilty for the tags she gives. It can't be shared. I feel the Sun has another task in mind for me."

The two friends brushed whiskers and hugged one another.

*

Chipling, tired after helping with the collection, burying and storing of the Autumn Harvest, found Marguerite one evening on the beach as the tide was going out. She was making patterns in the sand with her claws.

"Look at this," she said, pointing to where she had scratched a symbol A in the sand.

"What is it?" he asked.

"It's an A. A is for Acorn!"